When Angels

Sherryl D. Hancock

VULPINE
PRESS

Originally self-published by Sherryl D. Hancock in 2016

Published by Vulpine Press in the United Kingdom in 2017

ISBN 978-1-910780-34-3

Cover by Armend Meha

Cover photo credit: Tirzah D. Hancock

www.vulpine-press.com

Acknowledgements

Once again to our brave fighting troops for all that you do for your country and others, a very sincere Thank You. Post-Traumatic Stress Disorder is very real and needs to be addressed before things go too far awry. For all soldiers home from the war, **you are important, you are loved, and you are needed**. If you need help please call 1-800-273-8255 the Veterans Crisis Hotline. For more information and a great video on what this hotline does for Vets every day, check out the HBO Documentary: Crisis Hotline: Veterans Press 1. Please get help!

Also, to Google search for all the help and reference material.

This book is dedicated to Ralph W. Hancock Senior, a USAF veteran and my father-in-law, the very best man I've ever known. We miss you every day, Dad and think of you often. We love you and always will. Thank you for being the example of a man I can trust, I've encountered so few.

Chapter 1

"Hi, I'm Jams," said the handsome guy with the blue eyes, as he extended his hand to Devin. His eyes assessed her as he did.

Devin smiled, knowing she was being checked out and finding it endlessly amusing; she didn't date men. Her friends knew that, and yet they'd invited this guy and his friends to her party. It was her mistake, she'd told them to invite whoever they thought would be fun; maybe she needed to be more specific.

"Hi, make yourself at home," she said, gesturing at her Malibu home.

The house was beautiful, situated above the ocean, with an incredible view out every window. It was a party house, and everyone was making use of that. There was a large seating area with a widescreen TV that was running random movies. Music poured from hidden speakers throughout the house, a nice mixture of dance music, both new and old. A large bar held every manner of alcohol, while the huge commercial style fridge held beer, wine and soda.

As Devin moved on through the house, glancing around at the people gathered there, her eyes circled back to the man she'd just met, then skipped to his friends. That's when she saw her, the woman who stood with Jams and the other two men. Devin couldn't take her eyes off of her. The woman wasn't dressed outlandishly; in fact her clothing was very casual. But there was something about her that Devin couldn't quite place. She watched as the small group made its way over to some of the LAPD people that were there. So these people were fellow cops? Devin wasn't sure, but she planned to find out.

An hour later she'd been told that Jams and his 'crew' were actually part of the Los Angeles Fire Department Rescue team, they were a helicopter crew. Her eyes were drawn continually to the woman with the group, sensing easily that she was also gay. Devin wondered if that was why she was drawn to her. But that didn't really explain it, since there were a number of other lesbians at the party that Devin didn't know, but they weren't garnering as much of her attention.

Devin James always went with what felt right, and something was telling her that this woman was someone she wanted to know. So she planned to get to know her. As she made up her mind, she looked around to realize the woman had disappeared; she was no longer standing with her friends. She walked around the house having no luck locating her but just when she'd decided dejectedly that maybe the woman had left, she glanced out the back door. The woman was sitting in the backyard at one of the tables. She watched as the woman lifted a bottle of beer to her lips and glanced at her cell phone lying on the glass table next to her. Devin grinned as she saw the woman roll her eyes at the phone and push it farther away from her. The woman then reached over, took a cigarette out of the pack next to her and lifted it to her lips. She flicked open a Zippo lighter to light the end, and snapped it closed in one smooth motion. For some reason she couldn't put her finger on, Devin found the movement fascinating.

Opening the sliding door, Devin, stepped out into the backyard. The woman immediately glanced back at her, her impossibly light blue-green eyes narrowing slightly, as she blew a stream of smoke out from between her lips. Devin smiled, inclining her head as she moved to perch on a nearby chair.

"Are you not having a good time?" Devin asked, her eyes twinkling in amusement.

"Sure I am," the woman replied, her look direct as she lifted the beer to her lips again. She then leaned back comfortably, gesturing to the area around her. "This is some backyard."

Devin looked around her, grinning. "Yeah, I like it."

The phone on the table once again buzzed, eliciting a growl from the woman as she looked over at it again.

"Problems?" Devin asked.

The woman looked back at her. She sat back, taking a long draw off her cigarette. "Just stuff back home."

"And where is home?"

Light blue-green eyes narrowed slightly again, Devin could tell she was pushing her luck, but she was bound and determined to get to know this woman.

"Louisiana," the woman replied.

Devin nodded as if she understood. When further silence ensued, Devin pressed on.

"So, you're a friend of Jam's?"

The woman nodded.

Not exactly the expansive type is she? Devin thought to herself.

"He seems nice."

Devin saw the slight change in the other woman's demeanor; she stretched out her legs, looking down at the black combat style boots she wore, as she nodded. Then she looked back at Devin again.

"He's single," the woman said, as if confirming it for Devin.

It took Devin a second to realize that the woman obviously thought she was trying to pump her for information on Jams. She laughed nervously, shaking her head.

"Oh, no, I wasn't…" she began, almost comical in her quick denial of interest in Jams. She saw the other woman's lips tug in a grin at her discomfort, her light eyes twinkling humorously. It made Devin bold. "He's not my type… you are, though."

Devin wasn't sure why she got so much satisfaction out of the surprise that reflected in the other woman's eyes as she canted her head slightly. Even so, she only replied with a simple, "I see."

The woman was like Fort Knox! It had been years since Devin had to work this hard to hit on someone!

Unexpectedly, the sliding door opened and Jams stuck his head out the door. "Voodoo, get in here, we're doing shots!" he yelled gleefully.

The woman's reaction was to grin indulgently, shaking her head and glancing back at Jams. "In a minute," she replied, holding up her half-finished cigarette.

"Cool, cool!" Jams replied and went back inside.

There was a moment of silence as the two women regarded each other.

"Voodoo?" Devin asked her eyes alight with curiosity.

"Took about a second in flight school." When Devin looked mystified, she continued, "Your crew gives you your call sign. Louisiana, Voodoo, took seconds."

"Aw," Devin said, nodding her head and grinning, "so should I call you Voodoo?"

"Not if you want me to answer," the woman shot back, as if she'd said it a hundred times before.

Devin laughed at that response, then gave her a sidelong glance. "So what should I call you?"

The woman considered for a long moment, as if giving Devin her name would somehow violate some rule.

"Skyler."

"I'm Devin."

Skyler nodded, taking a long last draw on her cigarette as she stood up. Devin watched, thinking that Skyler was definitely attractive. She had a long lean frame. She wore faded blue jeans that clung nicely to her body, and a black tank top that exposed the lean muscle of her arms. Her dark hair was shoulder length and cut in short layers to frame a nicely tanned face and those hypnotic eyes, highlighted by thick black lashes. Devin found herself staring at Skyler's lips; they were full and sexy. Skyler wore very little makeup that Devin could detect, but she had such a beautiful face, no makeup really was needed to enhance her features.

Getting obsessed already, aren't we? Devin's mind told her.

She suddenly realized that Skyler was waiting for her to precede her back into the house, and chuckled nervously. Hopping off the chair she walked toward the slider.

Skyler watched the girl that she'd already deemed "the wild child," walk back into the house. Devin was definitely cute, with her black hair that was shot through with small sections of purple, and her very green eyes. There was no missing the great body on display either, with Devin's metallic black bikini top, and tattered jean shorts. She was all smooth skin and no visible tan lines. Skyler had taken note of the multiple piercings in Devin's ears too, as well as the one in her eyebrow.

In Skyler's opinion they were as opposite as night and day, and it had indeed shocked her when Devin had professed her interest. She hated to admit that it had her intrigued, to see the lengths this girl would go to in order to communicate with her. Most women didn't have that much energy. Skyler knew her mannerism was off-putting; it was intentional. And she only let people in that she wanted near her. There had been less and less people she wanted near her lately, it was concerning, but she wasn't thinking about that as she followed Devin back into the house.

"'Bout damned time!" Jams hollered, reaching over to hand Skyler a shot glass filled with a dark liquid.

Lifting his glass, Jams toasted somberly. "Angels fall."

Skyler inclined her head, and repeated, "Angels fall."

The other two crew members nodded too as they lifted their glasses and drank.

Devin looked on, curious about the toast; obviously it had a deep meaning to them. There was a lot more drinking and a few more interesting toasts, and it was becoming obvious that Skyler was getting a bit drunk. Devin started to detect a definite accent that she realized must be Cajun.

"No, no, no!" Skyler exclaimed at one point, holding up her hands for silence amongst the small group gathered around the bar. "What was dat, really?" she asked, her accent thicker now.

"Dat was a pass, cherie!" one of the other guys replied.

Skyler's look was stunned. Shaking her head she said, "Dat was de worst pass eva!"

"Maybe," Jams said, nodding his head in agreement, "but she's beatin' em off with a stick ladies and gentlemen!"

"Oh shut de hell up!" Skyler scowled, her eyes twinkled in amusement.

Devin looked on, watching the way that Skyler interacted with her team. It was very obvious that they'd been a group for a while, but the other two members, "Tom" and "Jerry" as they were nicknamed, were less familiar with Skyler than Jams was, and Devin wondered at that.

Skyler stepped back from the bar, picking up her bottle of beer, and reaching for her cigarettes and lighter.

"Cancer she is a callin'," she said, as she moved to the sliding glass door.

Five minutes later, Devin found Skyler in the exact spot she'd been in hours before. She grinned, noting that Skyler seemed much more relaxed this time, her legs stretched out in front of her and crossed at the ankles.

"And here you are again."

Skyler gave her a sidelong glance. "You allow smokin' in your house?"

"Nope."

"And das why I'm here again," Skyler replied smugly.

Devin nodded in acceptance. Reaching over, she pulled a chair up and sat down facing Skyler, her legs placed on either side of Skyler's outstretched legs. Skyler watched her warily, a wry grin on her lips, but she didn't shift her position.

"So," Devin began, as if to simply continue the conversation from much earlier in the evening. "What part of Louisiana are you from?" she asked, leaning forward, her eyes on Skyler's.

Skyler brought her cigarette up to take a long drag, considering Devon's question. Blowing smoke out in a long stream, she grinned, then nodded accepting that Devin was going to wait for the answer.

"Baton Rouge," Skyler said, but due to her accent it came out sounding like "bat ton rouge" with the "ton" emphasized heavily.

Devin stared back at her for a long moment, trying to decipher what she'd just been told. Skyler grinned, knowing she'd stumped the wild child for a moment at least.

"Is that Baton Rouge?" Devin asked finally, pronouncing it the way most American's would.

Skyler nodded, lifting her cigarette to her lips again. After taking a drag she rubbed her thumb under her lower lip; it was an action that those who knew her would recognize as her measuring how far she was going to let a person in. She didn't say anything else.

So still not a chatty Kathy, Devin thought to herself.

"And that's how the Cajun's say it?"

"Yes ma'am."

"Say it again," Devin said captivated.

8

Skyler looked amused by the request, but repeated the heavily accented "Baton Rouge" all the same.

"Very cool."

Skyler inclined her head, an amused smile on her lips, her eyes dancing in what Devin translated as a challenge of sorts.

"So, does drinking, bring out the accent?" Devin asked suddenly, breaking the silence that had begun to stretch.

"Pretty much."

"Do you drink a lot?" Devin asked, her looked direct and a bit challenging.

Skyler hesitated before she answered a bit defensively, "Sometimes."

Besides the tone of voice, Devin noted that Skyler also pulled her legs in and sat up a little straighter in her chair. Detecting a definite shift in the wrong direction, Devin decided to do something a little rash. Moving to stand, she stepped forward and leaned down, her face close to Skyler's.

"I like the accent," she whispered seductively, her lips right next to Skyler's ear.

Skyler shifted back just enough to look up into Devin's eyes.

"Do ya now?" Skyler asked huskily.

Devin nodded, her lips parting in response to the sudden surprising sexual tension that sprung up between them. As her eyes met Skyler's, she wondered if Skyler felt it too. Skyler's eyes flickered to Devin's lips then back up to meet her eyes again. It took a mere breath of movement and their lips met in a surprisingly hungry kiss.

Devin moved to straddle Skyler in the chair, as Skyler's hands slid into her hair, bringing her face closer, their lips never parting. The kiss intensified as their bodies pressed closer together. Devin grasped Skyler's shoulders amazed at her body's reaction. It had never been this intense before. There was no way she was going to stop now.

Skyler was letting the alcohol in her veins shut down all the warning bells that were trying to go off in her head. She told herself that for once she wasn't going to think; she was just going to let it happen. She wasn't sure her body would let her stop at that moment anyway, since every nerve she had seemed like it was a live wire suddenly.

They spent what seemed like hours exploring each other's mouths, hands grasping at hair and clothes. When things got decidedly more heated, Skyler moved to stand, lifting Devin up as she did and setting her gently on her feet. They stared at each other for a long moment; Devin took Skyler's hand in hers, turned and led her inside.

If anyone noticed the couple walking past them, they made no comment. Within moments Devin and Skyler were in a bedroom and there was no more hesitation. Clothing was quickly removed and tossed aside as they moved toward the bed. Their lips met once more, and neither of them spoke again. They communicated only through gasps, sighs, moans and quickened breathing. Afterwards, they both lay trying to catch their breath, the silence stretched, each of them thinking their own private thoughts.

Skyler knew she was making a mistake staying next to the black and purple haired vixen. Her mind had screamed at her so many times in the last few hours to get away from this girl. The minute Devin had told her that she was her type; she knew she should have made a quick getaway. Instead she'd stayed, relying on her ability to block any woman intent on getting close. What had she been thinking getting drunk around this woman? She had dropped her guard enough to let her get in, even just a little bit, and that had been all it took. *That and whatever spell she cast on me,* Skyler thought wryly, as her body slipped closer to sleep. The alcohol in her veins was sedating her, and her last thought and action before she slipped over that edge was to put space between herself and Devin's naked body lying next her. She'd already discovered that kissing this woman had been her undoing, keeping physical contact wasn't likely to be good either.

Devin felt Skyler moving away from her, she wondered at it, but decided she'd already pushed as much as she should with this woman. She didn't realize that the next morning she would wake up to find Skyler gone without a word.

Over the next week Devin waited to see if Skyler would contact her. She was disappointed, but not completely surprised when no contact came. Her ego was slightly assuaged when, at the end of the week, she heard that all of the LA Rescue people were up in Northern California helping out with wildfires that were burning out of control.

Devin gave it another week, then she heard the crews were returning to LA later that day. And when Skyler still hadn't reached out to contact her, she took matters into her own hands. She used her skills to find out where Skyler lived. It turned out that she lived in an upscale apartment in Van Nuys and apparently she and Jams were roommates. She found this last part out when he answered the door when she knocked.

"Hey," he said, grinning at her as he opened the door wider. She noted that he was wearing his flight suit, it was an army green color with an LA Fire Department patch on it.

"Come on in," he said, stepping back from the door. "We're just getting back."

"I heard you guys were up north," she said, stepping inside.

"We go where they tell us," he said. He gestured along the hallway. "She's down the hall, last door on the right."

Devin was surprised by the lack of preamble, like he'd been expecting her or at least wasn't surprised by her appearance.

What she didn't know was that he'd bugged Skyler about Devin endlessly while they'd been in Northern California. He'd asked her repeatedly if she planned on calling the girl. Skyler's replies had been less than friendly, though fortunately, he wasn't really afraid of his partner like others were. He watched Devin head toward Skyler's bedroom, grinning; the girl was definitely no wilting flower. He had a feeling Skyler had finally encountered someone she couldn't shut down so easily. He was happy about that.

Jams had known Skyler since they'd been in basic training together in the Army. They'd spent twelve years together, and he'd seen her through thick and thin. She'd dragged him through some pretty hard times in his life and career, and he trusted her with his life. He knew that Skyler was in a bad way right now, and he knew that something had to give at some point. He'd been waiting, with dread, for that breaking point. Part of him hoped that someone would come along that would be able to get through to his hardheaded partner; maybe Devin was that person. He didn't know, but he couldn't help but hope.

Devin noted that the door to Skyler's room was open. She peered inside and caught sight of Skyler standing with her back to the door. Skyler was still wearing her flight suit too, so Jams hadn't been exaggerating when he'd said they'd just gotten back. Devin hesitated, wondering if she should have waited a little bit longer before she decided to push Skyler again, but it was too late as Skyler turned around seeing her standing in the doorway. Devin couldn't help but notice that the flight suit Skyler wore was unzipped down to her waist, exposing a black sports bra and a lot of skin. She tried to concentrate on having a conversation with Skyler, and ignore her body's instant reaction to the image before her.

Skyler gave her a measuring stare, taking in the look of sudden desire on Devin's face, and clamped down on her instant response to it. *What is it about this girl?* Skyler thought, not for the first time in the last two weeks. It had definitely been easier to control her feelings when she wasn't in such close proximity to Devin; the memories weren't quite as vivid.

Leaning against the dresser behind her, Skyler placed her hands on either side of her, her look purposely bored. "What are you doing here?"

Devin stepped inside the door, tamping down on the irritation that rose at the sound of Skyler's tone.

"I hadn't heard from you. So I thought I'd come see if you were still alive."

Skyler nodded slowly, still assessing the situation. "I'm still alive."

Devin took a slow breath in through her nose, refusing to rise to the bait Skyler was throwing out, she was not going to scream at the other woman, no matter what.

"You didn't call," Devin said, hoping to sound conversational.

"Never said I would," Skyler replied expressionless.

Devin pursed her lips in consideration, then nodded. "You're right, you didn't but I hoped you would."

"Why?"

Devin looked back at her, surprised that someone could be so changeable. Staring back at Skyler she waited, and as she did, she caught a change in Skyler's look, her eyes dropped slightly. It was tiny; if she hadn't been looking right back at Skyler she wouldn't have seen it, but it showed that for all Skyler's bravado at that moment, there was something else going on. Devin just wasn't completely sure she knew what that something was, but she wanted to find out.

When Devin didn't answer, Skyler turned around and started taking off her watch and her necklace, placing them in a box on the dresser. She then moved to the bed and sat down to unlace her boots, glancing up at Devin, patiently waiting for an answer but refusing to ask the question again.

Devin looked back at the woman who'd been on her mind for the last two weeks, she was trying to decide how to answer Skyler's question. She wanted to scream at her, call her a bitch for making her a one-night stand, and for treating her like she was inconsequential. It was something she wouldn't normally stand for, but this was different. Skyler was different, and damn it, she wasn't going to just write this off.

As Skyler straightened from kicking off her boots, Devin caught the wary look in her eyes. Devin took a step closer to the bed in reaction and instantly saw Skyler's chin come up. Recognizing caution and even a slight note of alarm on Skyler's face, Devin knew what she needed to do. She walked straight over to Skyler, and stood right in front of her. Skyler's position on the bed put Devin above her. She heard Skyler's quick intake of breath and felt, rather than saw, her shift back slightly.

Skyler shuddered, feeling Devin's proximity send an electrical charge through her. Instantly all the sensations of their night together came rocketing back and she was trying desperately to hold onto her control. That was shattered a moment later when Devin uttered an, "Oh no you don't," and kissed her. Skyler let out a groan as she pulled Devin closer, deepening the kiss.

Devin's hands pushed at the flight suit, as she moved to straddle Skyler. Skyler obliged by pulling her arms out of the sleeves, then immediately put her arms back around Devin, keeping her close. Devin's nails bit into Skyler's arms as the heat between them intensified. Skyler shifted them back so she could lie back, taking Devin with her. Once again, clothes were removed and tossed aside and they were making love. It was another hour before they finally lay breathless on the bed.

Skyler lay with her body partially covering Devin's, her head on the pillow just above Devin's head. Devin had her hand on Skyler's arm that was across her body. It was a few minutes later when Devin felt Skyler start to shift away; she immediately tightened her hold on Skyler's arm. Skyler glanced down at her and Devin looked back at her with a challenge in her eyes.

Skyler actually laughed, surprising Devin completely.

"I can't run far," Skyler said in explanation. "I just didn't want to crush you."

Devin held onto Skyler's arm when she started to move back again. "I like you here."

"Yes, ma'am," Skyler said, grinning as she settled her body comfortably again.

They were both quiet for a while, but it was a comfortable silence. After a long while, Devin glanced up at Skyler. Sensing the movement, Skyler looked down at her. The sun was shining through the blinds in the room hitting Skyler's face, and it was then that Devin noticed how tired Skyler actually looked.

"When was the last time you slept?" she asked, concerned.

Skyler closed her eyes slowly, then opened them again. "I don't know. I can't ever sleep good on those fire lines."

"Why?" Devin asked, settling more comfortably to look up at Skyler.

"Well, we were in tents, and they don't stop flying out all night, so sleeping is rough. Plus, we worked twelve to fourteen hour shifts."

"Oh, my God. Okay, you need sleep." Devin said decisively.

"Not gonna argue," Skyler said, grinning, closing her eyes again, suddenly really starting to feel how tired she was.

"Oh happy day," Devin countered, grinning. "But when you wake up," she said, putting a finger to Skyler's chest, "I want to go back to my house."

Skyler looked mystified.

"I'm not leaving, until we leave together."

"Don't trust me, huh?"

"Not really, no," Devin confirmed.

Skyler nodded, accepting that. She knew her behavior had been reprehensible when it came to handling Devin's feelings, so she was willing to accept that blame. She still had no idea where this left them, but she was too tired to have that conversation at this point in time.

Skyler was asleep moments later, settled on her side. Devin moved to get up, putting her clothes on and wandering out of the room. She was surprised to see that Jams was still up and sitting at the dining room table eating, she'd expected him to be asleep in his room.

"Oh, hi," she said, as she walked into the dining room.

"Hey."

"I figured you'd be asleep like Skyler."

"Nah," he said, shaking his head. "I can sleep anywhere, it's a skill you learn in the Army."

"And Skyler didn't learn it?"

"She did," Jams said, his look changing slightly. "She just doesn't sleep as good as she used to."

Devin looked back at him for a long moment, waiting to see if he was going to elaborate, but he didn't.

He gave her a knowing grin. "So how's that goin'?" he asked, nodding his head toward Skyler's bedroom.

Devin moved to sit on the chair across from him, pulling her legs up and hugging her knees to her chest.

She shook her head in response to his question. "Does any woman ever know where she stands with her?"

"Not these days," he replied, with a pained look.

Devin knew there was more to that statement, but didn't feel like she had the right to ask at this point. In truth, she and Skyler were no closer to being in an actual relationship than they'd been an hour before. She'd just managed to confirm that Skyler's sexual attraction to her was just as strong as hers. She nodded, focusing on a thread on her jeans and toying with it.

"You need to know something," Jams said after a few long minutes, his tone serious.

"Okay…" Devin said cautiously.

"She has a lot going on," he said, putting his finger to his temple. "In here, you know?"

"I can see that."

"She really needs to work through some shit," Jams said, almost apologetic. "If she doesn't, it's not gonna be pretty."

Devin looked back at Skyler's friend, surprised by what he was telling her and unsure why he felt the need to say anything at all.

"Why are you telling me this?" she asked honestly.

He looked at her for a moment, his look as assessing as Skyler's had been earlier. Finally, he put his hand down on the table between them. "Because you're the first woman she's gotten this close to in two years."

"I don't know that where we've gotten is considered *close*."

"You've spent more than one night with her, that's closer than anyone else has gotten."

"Really?"

Jams made a sucking sound through his teeth. "Our girl doesn't usually get involved that fast, and she definitely doesn't respond to being pushed. You were pushing today by showing up here, and she usually pushes back."

"Oh, she did, trust me."

"But you're still here."

Devin looked back at him trying to detect any sort of ulterior motive, but she couldn't sense anything.

"How long have you known her?" she asked.

"Since basic," he answered, leaning back in his chair. "We met the first day. She was not one to be messed with, so I found it necessary to mess with her."

"How'd that go?"

"Knock down drag out fight by lunch, friends by dinner," he replied, grinning.

Devin laughed; it definitely sounded like the Skyler she knew so far. "How long ago was that?"

"Going on fifteen years."

"Wow!"

Jams nodded. "Yeah, long time."

Devin nodded too.

"Well," he said, standing up and picking up his plate. "I'm headed to the gym and then to see my girl. Feel free to hang out, raid the fridge, whatever."

"How do you know I'm not leaving?"

He gave her a sly look. "I think you're smarter than that," he said with a wink. With that he turned and walked out of the room.

Devin watched him go, shaking her head. Did he know Skyler that well? After fifteen years, she guessed he probably did. He left a short while later.

Devin retrieved her laptop from her car and did some work that she needed to catch up on. It was a few hours before she stood up to stretch. Walking around to restore some circulation to her legs, she started looking at some of the pictures that hung on walls in the living room. She also examined pictures that were propped on a long side table.

There were pictures of Jams with women, and pictures of him and Skyler, some in uniform, even one with them holding rifles in combat gear. There was even a picture of Skyler with a blond haired woman who she guessed Skyler must have been in a relationship with as they had the look of a couple.

Then she noticed that the fireplace mantle held three pictures, two of which had candles next to them. The center picture was of a crew stood in front of a helicopter, apparently Skyler and Jams' crew. She didn't recognize two of the men though, and they certainly weren't the two that had been with Skyler the night of the party. The two other pictures were single pictures of these same men. Devin realized that this was some kind of memorial .Then she thought about what Jams had said to her about "stuff" that Skyler needed to work through. Did this memorial have something to do with that statement? Reaching up, she touched the picture of the crew, as if it would somehow tell her what had happened.

"Hey," Skyler said from the living room doorway.

Devin looked back at her, seeing Skyler's eyes flick to the pictures she'd been examined, and then come back to her.

"Hi. You look better."

"Gee, thanks," Skyler replied, leaning against the door jam.

She wore jeans and a t-shirt that was emblazoned with "Army" in camouflage. Devin noticed Skyler's eyes skipped back to the picture again, it was obvious she was waiting for Devin to ask. Devin decided not to push. So she walked over, and leaned in to kiss Skyler's lips softly.

"Ready to get some dinner?" Skyler asked, seeming relieved that Devin hadn't asked any questions.

"Sure, yeah."

"Let me grab my keys."

"I have my car. I can drive, if you're still tired." Devin offered.

"Nah, I'm good. I know the area, probably better than you."

"Okay, true."

A few minutes later they walked out to the garage. Devin was not sure why she was surprised that Skyler's car was a sports car, she wasn't sure what she'd expected. It was a low-slung, sleek looking car, probably fast too. That bit did not surprise Devin at all.

"What is this?" she asked, as Skyler opened the passenger door for her.

"It's a Z," Skyler said, closing the door once Devin was seated, walking around to the driver's side.

Devin watched as Skyler pushed the ignition button and the engine roared to life with a throaty growl.

"Nice…" Devin said, sounding awed.

Skyler smiled proudly. "Yeah, isn't it?"

As Skyler pulled out of the garage and then gunned the engine, Devin was relieved for the seatbelt she had on, the car was indeed fast.

It definitely fit Skyler, the exterior was a pearlized white with red accents, and the interior was all race car, with rich black and red leather. She looked down at the floor mats and read the word stitched on them.

"What's Nismo?"

Skyler grinned as she gunned the engine to pass a number of cars. "It stands for Nissan Motorsports, it's a racing brand."

"So you have your own race car."

"I guess I have what's legal in a race car, yeah."

Skyler reached over and turned on the stereo. Devin was not surprised when rock music flowed out of the speakers. She recognized the band as Rush, it seemed to fit Skyler's style. They rode for a little while, Devin watching Skyler drive.

Skyler had one hand on the steering wheel, the other hand on the stick shift. She was tapping the stick shift to the drum beat of the song that was on: Billy Squire's "Everyone Wants You." Devin noticed the ring she wore on her right ring finger, it looked like a class ring, but she could see that it said "ARMY" on it.

The song on the stereo changed, and Devin noticed immediately that Skyler's mood did as well; it was like she went into a trance, even as she reached over to turn the song up. Devin glanced at the display and noticed the song was called "Angels Fall." She immediately recalled the odd toast that Skyler and Jams had done at the party, and she wondered if the song had anything to do with that toast. Minutes later she was sure she knew.

Glancing at Skyler, Devin could see the faraway and devastated look on her face, even though her eyes were hidden by sunglasses. Devin listened to the words of the song looking for a clue as to what was causing the change in mood. The first lines of the song were grave, talking about giving up a fight, the words sounded like an anthem to depression or even suicide, which surprised Devin greatly.

Skyler sang along to the chorus with feeling; the words were crushing. They talked about angels falling with broken wings. It had a very definite sense of hopelessness to it, and Devin wondered how close to reality those words were for Skyler.

Devin glanced at Skyler's hand on the stick shift, noticing that Skyler's thumb was rubbing at the underside of the Army ring in agitation. Devin knew this was somehow very important and it was taking everything she had not to ask anything. When the song ended Skyler reached over and turned the radio back down as another song began. She glanced out the driver's window, reaching up quickly to brush at the corner of her eyes, which Devin suspected was a tear. When Skyler placed her hand back on the stick shift, as they drew up to a red light, Devin reached out taking Skyler's hand in hers, her finger touching the ring. Taking the moment to look at the ring more closely she read the words engraved on either side.

"Fifty-ninth Angels?" she asked softly, glancing over at Skyler, whose face could have been carved out of stone. Skyler's hand closed in an instant reaction to the words Devin had just spoken.

Pulling her hand away, Skyler rubbed the bridge of her nose with her index finger. "It's a unit thing."

Devin looked back at her for a long time, hoping she'd explain. She didn't. Devin was sure she'd just seen the tip of the iceberg and it made her ache for this woman. She wasn't sure if she was right about what she was guessing, but if she was, Skyler had at the very least, lost someone in the war. She guessed two members of her own crew. The idea was so sad to Devin that she had to force back the desire to cry.

Skyler could detect Devin's empathy and she steeled herself against it, snapping her mind shut on the ache she felt through every fiber of her being. *Not now!* she told herself firmly. She'd been surprised to hear the song. It had been awhile, and she hadn't had the heart to turn it off, she never could. She let the pain rip through her every time she heard it; it was like penance to her. However, she'd never meant to let Devin or anyone else see that part of her self-punishment, she rarely even let Jams see it and he'd been there when it happened. *Not now, not now,* she chanted in her head, willing away the desire to scream and just veer into oncoming traffic to finally end the torture.

When they got to the restaurant, Skyler asked Devin to go get a table, and said she'd meet her inside. Devin nodded, knowing this wasn't the time to push and went inside. Outside, Skyler paced agitatedly, chain-smoking three cigarettes before she could calm herself again. Somewhere in a small corner of her mind, she knew that things were getting worse, but it wasn't a corner she was willing to look into at that moment.

When she finally joined Devin in the restaurant she was calm again.

"Sorry," she apologized as she sat down.

"It's okay. Are you okay?" Devin asked gently.

Skyler took a deep breath, expelled it and nodded. "Yeah."

Devin wasn't convinced, but she'd already decided she needed to leave things alone for the moment. They weren't even close to being on a familiar enough footing for her to question Skyler about something so significant. Devin knew that what she'd just witnessed in the car had been part of what Jams had tried to warn her about. It also had something to do with the pictures on the mantelpiece. The part of her that loved to solve mysteries and fix things whenever she could was itching to know, to ask everything she could, but these were Skyler's feelings, not machines and she knew she needed to take it slow.

After they'd ordered, Skyler sat back in her chair looking over at her.

"So," she said, her tone casual. "You know what I do for a living, but I don't know what you do there at the LAPD so..."

"Oh, I don't work for the LAPD. I'm a consultant."

Skyler looked back at her, grinning slightly, with a look in her eyes that Devin didn't understand. "So what do you consult on?"

Devin hesitated, trying to figure out the look of amusement in those beautiful eyes. "I basically work with computers."

"What do you do with computers?"

"I guess you could say I fix them," Devin replied.

"You fix them. Huh, is that the story you want to stick with?"

Devin knew she was walking into a trap, but she nodded anyway.

"So, do you use that PhD you have from MIT to *fix them*?" Skyler asked, widening her eyes like she was saying, *caught ya.*

Devin's mouth dropped open in surprise. "How do you know that?"

"How did you know where I live?"

Devin pulled herself up short, her chin coming up slightly at being challenged, but then she started to grin as she inclined her head. "You got me there."

Skyler chuckled, looking pleased with herself.

"So I have a degree, big deal. I'd bet my life you have one too," Devin said.

Skyler sat back, grinning indulgently. "What makes you think that?"

Devin gave her a sour look, even as her eyes danced with humor; she was thoroughly enjoying this banter, and was thrilled that Skyler was finally talking to her openly.

"Well, I know that to be a pilot in the military you have to be an officer, and officers have to have a degree," she said triumphantly.

Skyler looked back at her, the grin not leaving her lips, which told Devin she'd made a mistake somewhere in that statement. "Except for the Army. They don't require helicopter pilots to be either officers or have a degree."

"Seriously?" Devin asked, not sure if Skyler was just messing with her.

"Yeah, it's called high school to flight school."

"Son of a…"

Skyler chuckled. "I do, however, have a degree."

"You brat!" Devin exclaimed, tossing her napkin at Skyler.

Skyler laughed ducking the napkin. "I never said I didn't, I just wanted to know what made you so sure I had one."

Devin shook her head, holding up her hand in the classic "talk to the hand" gesture. Skyler laughed, enjoying their conversation and feeling more relaxed than she had in a long time.

"So what's your degree in?" Devin asked.

"Aeronautics."

"Wow," Devin said, impressed. "What level?"

Skyler looked back at her, grinning again. "Well, it's not a PhD."

Devin narrowed her eyes. "Then what is it?"

Skyler laughed, holding up her hands to ward off the threat she was seeing in the other woman's eyes. "It's a masters, but not from somewhere like MIT."

"Oh, whatever!" Devin said, making a face, and shaking her head. "So what made you want to be a pilot?"

"I actually originally didn't," Skyler said, smiling at the waitress as she brought their food.

Devin thanked the waitress as she left, looking over at Skyler as she picked up her fork. "So what made you decide?"

"Well, both Jams and I scored high on our ASVABs."

"What's an ASVAB?"

"It's the test they give you when you go into the military, it tells the military where your strengths lie. Basically, if you want to be a pilot, you have to do well on the Flight Aptitude part of the tests. Jams and I both did, and when they told us we didn't have to be officers, I told Jams we needed to do it. I knew he wanted to be like his dad. He was an Army pilot too, and I wasn't going to let him do it without me."

"Really? But you're his boss, aren't you?"

Skyler shrugged. "Yeah, I guess I'm just better at it than him."

"Uh-huh," Devin said, grinning and suspecting that Skyler was downplaying her skills. "You sure aren't the cocky pilot type, are you?"

"Nah, I leave that to the guys."

"You don't use it to pick up women?"

"Did I use it to pick you up?" Skyler asked.

"You didn't pick me up, I picked you up," Devin countered.

Skyler laughed, nodding her head. "Yes you did and I still haven't figured out why."

"Why I picked you up?"

"Yeah, even when I did everything to keep you from doing just that."

"Why did you want to keep me from picking you up?" Devin asked, her tone casual. She hoped Skyler would be honest.

Skyler looked back at her considering. "It's easier not to get involved."

"Why do you want easy?"

"'Cause everything else is hard right now," Skyler replied, her tone was even, but Devin saw a look in her eyes that told her that Skyler was testing her.

Devin wondered at that and she wasn't sure, but she got the feeling that if she dove into asking questions right then, Skyler would back up. Maybe that's what she wanted.

Little did Devin know how right she was. The direction of the conversation had strayed into dangerous territory and Skyler was hoping to have a reason to back up again. If Devin pushed, there would be push back.

Devin nodded, not asking any questions about the statement. Their dinner continued and they discussed other things, avoiding the topic of their first meeting.

Later, on the way back to Skyler's apartment they discussed how they would arrange the trip over to Devin's house.

"I'll just grab some stuff and head over," Skyler said.

Devin gave her a measuring look. "And you'll come over tonight?"

Skyler looked over at her, recognizing the hesitation in Devin's voice. "Do you want me to come over tonight?"

"Yes."

Skyler smiled, the girl didn't seem to have much guile about her. "Then I'll come over tonight."

"Okay," Devin said, satisfied. "Then you can just drop me off at my car."

They pulled into the lot at the apartments. "Which one is it?"

"That one there," Devin said pointing. "The Hummer."

Skyler burst out laughing. "Seriously?"

Devin smiled, recognizing the irony of someone of her small stature, only five foot four, driving such a big vehicle, she'd heard it enough from others.

"Don't start with me," Devin said, amused. "I didn't give you a hard time about your own personal jet here."

"True. You win this round."

Devin laughed. "Yay me."

Skyler grinned, then leaned over kissing Devin's lips. "I'll be there in an hour or so, okay?"

"You remember where it is?"

"Huge house in Malibu. The house that MIT built."

"Stop it," Devin said, detecting the teasing in Skyler's tone.

Skyler laughed as Devin got out of the car.

True to her word, an hour later, Skyler rang the bell at Devin's house.

Chapter 2

Devin and Skyler spent the next three days together at Devin's house, spending a lot of that time in bed. In between, Skyler was usually out in Devin's backyard. On the third morning, Devin found her sat outside first thing. Skyler was smoking and had a cup of coffee next to her on the table. She was sitting with her legs extended in front of her, her bare feet on the chair across from her.

"Am I always going to find you out here?" Devin asked as she walked out the door.

Skyler glanced at her over her shoulder, grinning. "You ever going to allow me to smoke in your house?"

"Nope."

"Then you're always going to find me out here," Skyler replied with a nod, as she moved her feet to let Devin sit down.

Devin sat in the chair, and took Skyler's feet and pulled them back onto her lap, her hands caressing them. Skyler watched the action, her look soft. Devin really liked Skyler's personality; she was sometimes very quiet and contemplative, and then other times she could be outgoing, funny and smart with a quick wit. It was a nice balance.

They sat in silence for a bit, enjoying the sound of the ocean far below, and the sounds of birds calling to each other. It was a nice morning with the slightest chill to it. Skyler liked that Devin was willing to just sit quietly at times. Too often, women felt like they needed to fill silence with something so they chattered, sometimes incessantly. It drove Skyler crazy. Devin was definitely high energy, but it was a relief to find that she could also contain that energy when the need arose.

After a while, Skyler leaned her head back on her chair, drawing in a deep breath, then looked over at Devin. "Have I mentioned how much I like your backyard?"

"You did tell me that the first night we met."

"Well, I'm telling you again, this backyard is awesome."

Devin smiled, liking the compliment. "Well, it's nothing like what I grew up with. When I could afford it, I wanted something like this."

"So where did you grow up?"

"Here in LA. Definitely not in Malibu, though."

"So where?"

"In Compton."

"Holy shit," Skyler replied, shocked. "Tough neighborhood."

"You said it. I was one of the few white girls in the apartments we lived in."

"That was rough, I'm sure," Skyler said, already reevaluating this woman.

Devin shrugged. "I'm nothing if not adaptable."

"That's pretty adaptable," Skyler said, shaking her head.

"What about you?" Devin asked. "What was it like growing up in Baton Rouge?"

"It wasn't LA that's for sure."

"What did your parents do?" Devin asked, leaned back, getting comfortable.

"Blue-collar, both of them. Dad worked at a chemical company and mom cleaned houses south of Florida Boulevard."

"What does that mean? South of Florida Boulevard?"

Taking a long drag off her cigarette, Skyler grinned. "That's where the rich people live in Baton Rouge."

"Oh." Devin replied, a little sheepish. "So you left there when you were how old?"

"The minute I turned eighteen and could join the Army."

"Wow, really?"

"Hell yeah, I hated Baton Rouge, and it wasn't fond of me either," Skyler replied.

"Why did you hate it?"

"Well, they don't cotton to gay people, real well there." Skyler said sourly.

"You knew were gay then?"

"I pretty much always knew I was gay," Skyler said. "I hung out with boys, I wasn't interested in any of them. The girls that came around though…"

"Oh, ho…" Devin laughed. "I see. I didn't figure it out until I was in college."

"Late bloomer."

"Wasn't that hard for you, though? Being gay in the Army? That was during Don't Ask, Don't Tell, wasn't it?"

Skyler coughed. "Uh, before it, actually."

"Oh, wow," Devin said, shaking her head. "I've never understood that whole thing, it was just stupid and Don't Ask Don't Tell just made it worse."

"Dated a few military women, have we?"

"A couple."

"Uh-huh," Skyler said, giving her a mockingly suspicious look.

"I was usually safer for a lot of them, since I had a place far from the city, and I was a civilian and all."

"Right," Skyler said, with a sarcastic roll of her eyes. "Had nothing to do with you being hot."

"You think I'm hot?"

Skyler stared at her in disbelief. "You can't tell that I think you're hot?"

Devin gave her a sidelong look. "You're not exactly an open book, Sky."

Skyler wondered why the shortened version of her name sounded so good coming out of Devin's mouth. Crushing out her cigarette, she moved to stand, reaching out and taking Devin's hand pulling her up too. Staring down into Devin's emerald green eyes, she leaned down and kissed her deeply on the lips, pulling her closer.

Looking down into Devin's eyes again, she said, "I think you're incredibly hot."

"Mmm," Devin murmured, reaching up to pull Skyler's head back down to her and returning the deep kiss, letting her hands trail up through Skyler's hair.

Minutes later they were in the house, making love on the couch. The rest of the day was spent watching movies, and making love whenever they felt like it.

"So, how's it going with the hot doctor?" Jams asked the next day when Skyler arrived at the hangar.

Skyler merely smiled widely, her eyes twinkling.

"That good, huh?"

It was good to see Skyler smile for a change. It had been so long since she'd been happy and Jams had begun to wonder if she'd ever be happy again. He knew he was getting his hopes up with this new relationship, but it was worth the even temporary relief it brought.

Their day was spent doing engine checks and maintenance reports for the helicopters. The minute their time was done, Skyler was in her car and flipping him a wave as she drove off. He watched smiling.

"What's this?" Devin asked later that evening as they lay in bed at her house. Her finger was brushing a scar on Skyler's chest.

She didn't notice Skyler tense, but she heard the tension in her voice when she answered.

"It's from a crash."

Devin moved to lean up on her elbow, looking up at Skyler, seeing the muscle in her jaw jumping as she clenched her teeth, her eyes like ice.

"When?"

Skyler's eyes narrowed slightly and Devin feel Skyler wanting to move away, even though she didn't actually move.

"Two and a half years ago."

Devin hesitated. "Bad?"

"Not good," Skyler said, incredulously.

Devin shuddered at the combination of Skyler's tone and the look on her face. "You think I'm pushing."

"I think you're pushing."

Devin drew in a deep breath, and nodded almost to herself. Getting up and stretching she walked toward her bathroom. Over her shoulder she said, "I'm going to take a shower."

Skyler lay in bed, watching the doorway Devin had disappeared into. Reaching up she rubbed her lower lip with her thumb, her eyes narrowing as her mind did it's best to put away the tension she'd been feeling moments before.

Devin was washing her hair, eyes closed, when she heard the shower door open. She rinsed the soap out of her hair, then wiped the water out of her eyes, just as Skyler's lips touched hers. It was a soft, sweet kiss, an "I'm sorry" kiss. Devin wound her arms around Skyler's neck, kissing her back, and doing her best to show her that she accepted the apology.

Later that night, though, as Skyler lay sleeping in bed, Devin snuck out of the bedroom and did what she'd been trying to avoid doing; she used her formidable skills to track down information about Skyler and her crew, using what little she knew about them. It took a while and bending a few federal information technology laws but she finally found what she'd been looking for. She read the redacted report of the accident that the Black Hawk fifty-nine of the third Assault Helicopter battalion had been in over Iraqi soil. There wasn't a lot of information, but what she read made her feel sick to her stomach. The report outlined how the Black Hawk was hit by machine-gun fire that damaged the tail rotor of the aircraft, and sent it spinning out of control. It was noted that Chief Warrant Officer Five, Skyler Boché and copilot Chief Warrant Officer Four, Daniel Lauret, who Devin assumed was Jams, controlled the spin, but the helicopter was hit again with fire and finally succumbed to its damages. Staff Sergeant Tom O'Reilly was killed in the crash.

Then there were several lines blacked out in the report, but Devin was able to determine that somewhere along the way Staff Sergeant Billy Kings was also killed. It was listed that CWO5 Boché sustained multiple injuries including two gunshot wounds, a head injury, thoracic trauma, four broken ribs, and a punctured lung. It also listed that CWO4 Lauret sustained two gunshot wounds as well as head trauma from the crash. Devin noted that much of the report was blacked out, and she was curious to know what was behind those solid black lines. She was sure it had a lot to do with Skyler's current mental state.

Devin hadn't realized she was crying until she finally closed the report and backed out of the website she'd found it on, covering her electronic tracks as she did. She sat at her computer for a long time, just trying to imagine what it would have been like to be in a crash like that. And what about the gunshot wounds? Had they happened when the helicopter was being fired at? Or had they happened after it crashed? It gnawed at Devin, her mind thinking a million things, as she went back into the bedroom to see Skyler asleep, lying naked from the waist up, her arm thrown above her head. It was then, in the light of the doorway, that Devin started to see the small scars on Skyler's chest, even one just below her shoulder. Devin wondered why she hadn't noticed them before. Now she couldn't stop thinking about what had happened in Iraq, and how this woman was possibly affected by the crash.

Skyler stirred, opening her eyes and seeing Devin standing next to the bed looking devastated. Moving slowly to sit up, Skyler pulled the sheet up to cover herself, as she saw Devin's eyes move to her shoulder.

Devin saw Skyler's chin come up, and she knew then that Skyler had sensed her fear and worry. She tried to cover it quickly.

"Sorry," she said, smiling. She walked back to the bathroom to turn the light off. "I didn't mean to wake you."

When she turned around she knew her attempt at hiding her churning emotions hadn't been successful. She sat down on the bed, and winced as Skyler moved away from her, her eyes narrowed.

"You did it, didn't you?" Skyler said, her tone accusing.

"Skyler…"

"You fucking hacked it, didn't you?" Skyler asked angrily.

Devin debated lying to her, wanting to take that look of betrayal out of Skyler's eyes, but she knew lying would be worse.

"Yes, I looked it up," Devin said, finally. "I knew if I asked you that you wouldn't tell me, and honestly I didn't want to hurt you by asking."

Skyler's look did not change, but her jaw tightened noticeably.

"So what do you think you know now?" she asked.

Devin looked back at this woman who'd been so sweet just hours before, realizing that she may have just made a serious mistake. It was too late.

"Skyler..." Devin began trying to reason, but Skyler wasn't having it.

"What do you think you know?" Skyler repeated, her words measured and biting this time.

Devin swallowed, blowing her breath out slowly. "That the Black Hawk you were piloting in Iraq crashed and—"

"Was shot down," Skyler inserted sharply.

Devin blinked a couple of times, knowing there was no way out of this and just wanting to get through it.

"Was shot down, and that you and Jams were both hurt badly..." Her voice trailed off as tears clogged her throat suddenly.

Skyler's eyes took on an edge, her face a mask of disgust. "And two of my crew were killed."

Tears slid from Devin's eyes as she nodded.

"Say it!"

"And two of your crew were killed," Devin said quietly.

"Is that what you needed to know?" Skyler shouted, getting out of the bed, and pulling on her clothes.

Devin watched helplessly, crying softly as Skyler dressed.

Skyler threw an angry look over her shoulder; she felt as if someone had just punched her in the stomach. In the moonlight coming through the bedroom windows she could see Devin crying. It wasn't a wailing 'give me attention' kind of cry, but a devastated brokenhearted kind of cry. Skyler closed her eyes, trying with every fiber of her being to shove down the fury she'd been feeling moments before. Breathing slowly, she willed herself to calm down. Turning around, she stood looking at Devin for a long minute. Finally, she walked around the bed, sitting beside Devin, pulling her into her arms. Devin buried her face in Skyler's shirt, her arms wound around Skyler's waist as she did her best to stop crying.

Finally, Devin raised her eyes to Skyler. "I'm sorry," she said, her tone devastated. "I didn't mean to hurt you, please don't leave."

Skyler looked down at her, her eyes searching Devin's. She knew she'd overreacted, and she knew that it was just this kind of rage that had ended a previously long relationship. While she was nowhere near ready to deal with all the aspects of the crash, she also knew it was her own refusal to discuss it that had forced Devin to try to find out on her own.

"I can't talk about it," Skyler said, her tone apologetic. "Not yet, maybe not ever."

Devin nodded, sniffing and reaching up to wipe away tears.

"Okay," she said softly, "I'm really sorry."

Skyler grimaced. "No, I'm sorry, Devin, it wasn't fair to try to keep the whole thing away from you, it forced you to do what you did. I shouldn't have yelled, so I'm sorry."

Reaching up, Skyler's fingers brushed away the last of the tears on Devin's cheek. Leaning down she kissed Devin's lips softly. *Two apologies in less than two hours*, Skyler thought, *it's becoming a damned epidemic.*

The next day they were in Devin's bathroom getting ready for work when Skyler's phone buzzed. She picked it up looking at the message.

"Aw, damn it," she said, sending a text.

"What?" Devin asked, glancing at her in the mirror.

"I forgot Jams' parents are coming today."

"Is that bad?" Devin asked, turning to face Skyler.

"No," Skyler said, shaking her head. "It just means I've been too distracted with a particularly hot PhD."

"Oh, so now it's my fault?"

Skyler stepped over to lean down and kiss her on the lips. "You do keep me distracted."

"Well, if it's a problem…" Devin replied, stepping back.

Skyler laughed, grabbing her around the waist and pulling her back. "I don't think so," she said, kissing her again.

Devin was relieved that Skyler was back to normal this morning; she'd been so afraid the night before that she'd pushed things too far, and she was going to lose the connection with this woman. She still wasn't sure what had drawn them together, but she had a feeling it had everything to do with the crash, and Devin really wanted to be there for Skyler when she finally dealt with whatever demons still haunted her.

After kissing for a few minutes they went back to getting ready. Skyler watched as Devin put on her makeup, glancing at her phone and answering messages as she did. Skyler was fascinated with the process Devin went through to get ready to go to work; hair, makeup, outfit, and not just clothes coordinated but accessories, earrings, watch and bracelets too. To Skyler the process was exhausting, but she had to admit the final product was amazing.

Devin had a style all her own. Regular clothes weren't her thing, she liked quirky interesting pieces, like a great pair of shoes, and she'd build an entire outfit around them. Everything coordinated, right down to the color of eye shadow she wore; it was something that defined her in other people's heads. She was quirky, but put together in a way that a lot of people couldn't really explain even if they tried. Most people just thought of her as a dynamic fireball of a person, and when she got to work on solving their problems with their systems, no one expected her to be as good as she was.

In Devin's world, she was a goddess. Computer programmers would consider her area of expertise as a hacker, and she was good at it. She was able to track down viruses and malicious software in systems, and was able to track them back to their origin. Law enforcement agencies all over the country knew about her, and contacted her when they had breaches in their systems, or needed her assistance on high profile cases. She was a hot, and therefore expensive, commodity, so she was contacted when only the best would do. She had a reputation in the industry, and was often referred to as "The Glimmer" for her ability to completely erase her digital footprint from a system once she'd been there.

Skyler and Devin had discussed it one night as they lay in bed.

"Why haven't you told me this up until now?" Skyler had asked, her fingers intertwined with Devin's.

Devin had shrugged, glancing back at Skyler. They were lying on their backs, Devin's head had been in the hollow of Skyler's shoulder, Skyler's arm under her neck, holding her hand.

"What was I supposed to say?" Devin had asked. "Hi, I'm a super hacker?"

Skyler grinned. "Maybe?"

"Uh-no."

"You could have told me you're a very successful computer consultant."

Devin had moved to turn over on her stomach, levering herself up on her elbows and looking down at Skyler. "So, 'Hi, I'm a super hacker who doesn't even get out of bed for less than a hundred thousand'?"

Skyler had given her a stunned look. "A hundred thousand dollars?"

Devin had laughed, nodding.

"Son of a…" Skyler had muttered in shock.

Now watching Devin get ready, Skyler was still astounded at how much Devin made doing her job. It definitely explained the house she owned because houses in Malibu were not cheap, and Devin's was just incredible. In comparison, rescue chopper pilots didn't make anywhere near as much. It was a decent living, but was nowhere near what Devin made. Skyler guessed that she better to let go of the antiquated idea that she should make more than someone she was dating.

"So, Jams' parents?" Devin asked, leading.

"Are awesome. They own a farm in Kansas now, but Jams' dad was an Army pilot too."

"Oh, yeah, I remember now. So Jams is just carrying on tradition."

"Yeah, but he really didn't think he was going to make it as a pilot, he didn't think he had the knack for it."

"Does he?"

"He's good…"

"But?" Devin asked, hearing the hesitation in Skyler's voice.

"But, I think he does it more for his dad than for him."

"Oh, that's rough. My parents wanted me to do more than what I am too."

Skyler gave her a deadpan look. "They want you to make more than 'no less than a hundred thousand dollars' a job?"

Devin laughed, knowing she was never going to hear the end of that statement. "No, they don't like what I do. They think it's somehow unsavory."

"Seriously?" Skyler asked, thinking of what Devin had said about growing up in Compton and wondering how parents from there could hold themselves so high above what their daughter did.

"My mom's a teacher, in one of the worst schools in Compton, and my dad works with a non-profit," Devin said.

"So they don't like that you're taking so much money for what you do?" Skyler practically glowered. "Do they want you to be poor and live in Compton with them?"

Devin bit her lip, enjoying the loyalty she could hear in Skyler's voice. "Well, they don't live in Compton itself anymore, but I'm sure they'd like me to do something more 'service oriented.'"

Skyler made a dismissive "Pfft" sound with her mouth. "It ain't like you're working with the big corporations to figure out how to rip off the little guy. Jesus!"

Devin laughed. "It doesn't matter to me. I went to MIT to make them happy, and I do what I do for a living to make me happy."

"Good," Skyler said with finality.

"So are you close to Jams' parents?" Devin asked, getting the conversation back to Skyler, who always seemed to find a way to steer it away from herself.

Skyler looked back at her, narrowing her eyes slightly, meaning she knew what Devin was doing, but she didn't comment on it.

"Yeah, I am," she said. "They are really great, and have been there for me like my parents never were."

Devin nodded, now very interested in meeting these people.

Later, Skyler drove them to work; Devin was still working with the LAPD on a job, so they were headed to the same area.

"So, we'll probably have dinner with Jams' parents tonight, are you okay with that?" Skyler asked.

Devin checked her calendar on her phone and nodded. "Yeah, I should be able to, I just need to move a meeting."

"If you can't make it, it's okay," Skyler said, not wanting to interfere with Devin's schedule.

"I'll make it."

"Okay," Skyler replied equally serious, yet grinning.

At the hangar, Jams said that they needed to leave at three o'clock to pick his parents up at the airport.

"Got it," Skyler nodded, as she continued to work on the log for the maintenance they'd performed the day before.

They had a maintenance crew, but there were certain things that Skyler felt the need to check on and handle herself. The maintenance crew chief knew her well enough to trust her skills.

"They're going to want to meet Devin, you know," Jams said, his tone conversational.

Skyler glanced up at him. "Is that your way of warning me that you've already told them about her?"

"You know they always want to know how you're doing."

"Uh-huh," Skyler muttered, giving him a suspicious look. "Did you call them that first night from the party?"

Jams laughed, shaking his head. "Nah, just the day that she showed up at the apartment to kick your ass."

Skyler gave him a withering look. "I already told her that we'd be having dinner with your parents tonight, smart ass."

"Better than being a dumb ass."

"Yeah, yeah," Skyler retorted, going back to her report.

Jams had indeed told his parents about Devin. They were constantly worried about Skyler, and he was happy to give them good news about Skyler finally finding someone again. His parents were thrilled and had told him to make sure they got to meet this young lady when they were in town.

That afternoon there were hugs all around when Skyler and Jams picked up his parents.

Jams' mother, Helen, held Skyler's face in her hands for a long minute. "You look better."

"She'd have to," put in Jams' father, Roy.

Skyler took it all in, these were people she respected, much more than she did her own parents. For them to be so concerned about her, touched her heart.

"Thanks," Skyler smiled.

"You still look too skinny though," Helen said.

"You always say that! And I keep telling you that this is just how I am."

"Yeah, yeah," Helen said, waving away Skyler's comment. "If you eat more, you'll gain weight."

"I don't know, mom, she eats a lot," Jams said, with a snide grin.

"At least I always made weight," Skyler said, referring to the weight requirements for soldiers in the Army.

"Oh…" Roy said, grinning. "She's got you there son."

"It was baby fat," Jams said, as they all turned to walk to the baggage claim. "Wasn't it mom?"

"Of course, honey," Helen said, always indulgent of her boy.

"See? Mom said!" Jams said, like a little kid.

"She has to, it's her job," Skyler replied, sticking her tongue out at him.

The four of them laughed as they reached the baggage claim.

On the way back to the apartment they talked about the sleeping arrangements, since all Jams had told his parents was that they didn't need to make a hotel reservation.

"You're gonna sleep in Sky's room," Jams said.

"We don't want to put you out, girl," Roy said.

"You aren't putting her out Dad," Jams put in before Skyler could answer. "She stays at Devin's house in Malibu most of the time these days."

"In Malibu?" Helen asked surprised. "Isn't that where movie stars live?"

Skyler grinned. "Yeah, some do. Devin's a computer consultant."

"And she makes bank!" Jams said.

"What does that mean?" Roy asked his son.

"It means she makes a lot of money, Dad. Her house is, what… Sky, a cool three mill at least?"

Skyler gave him a narrowed look. "Not that it's any of our business. But yeah, it's pretty nice, and I'm sure it cost a good amount."

"Daniel," Helen said, her tone scolding. "That is none of your business. I raised you better than that."

"Yes ma'am," Jams answered his mother, ever the obedient boy.

Skyler looked over at her partner, delighting in the uncomfortable look he had on his face now. He gave her a foul look. Just then their pagers went off. Checking hers, Skyler looked over at Jams.

"Damn it," Jams said, knowing what it meant. "Mom, Dad, I gotta drop you off at the apartment, then we gotta go back to work, we have a mission."

"Don't worry about it," Roy said. "The job comes first."

Fortunately, the mission they were called in for was canceled last minute. They were able to keep their plans and go to dinner with Jams' parents. Skyler left the hangar to pick up Devin saying she'd meet them at the restaurant.

Jams went home to pick up his parents. On the way to the restaurant Roy and Helen questioned him on how Skyler was handling things these days.

"She's still having a rough time of it," Jams told his parents honestly. "And I worry about her."

Roy nodded. "A crash is a hard enough thing to recover from, but the rest... that's gonna take some time."

Jams nodded. "I know, Dad, but there's times when I just don't know how long she'll hang in there, and she isn't dealing with it."

"That's not good," Helen said from the back seat.

"What about this new girl?" Roy asked. "Is she likely to help?"

"I think so. Sky is really into her and I think that's going to give her some motivation to handle things, at least, more than she has done so far."

"What do you mean?" Helen asked.

"Well, this girl isn't the kind of woman that Skyler usually dates, at least not the type she's... uh... been with lately."

Jams found himself trying to be delicate about the subject of Skyler's one-night stands.

"What does that mean, young man? Is she sleeping around?" Helen asked, her Bible belt thinking coming out suddenly.

Roy and Helen were devout Christians, and when their son brought home the woman he called his best friend, they were sure she was his girlfriend. He explained quickly that she was not his girlfriend and that she didn't actually date men at all. They had been surprised by this information, and it wasn't something they easily understood, having not been exposed to many people in the gay community. What they did understand about Skyler Boché was that she was a good influence on their son. When Daniel had left for the Army, it was with the attitude that he'd do his four years and then get out. He'd had no goals, no real plans. It was Skyler who had encouraged him to apply for flight school when they'd both done well on their ASVABs. Roy was eternally grateful to Skyler for getting his son to consider flight school. He didn't care what her sexual preference was, she was a good person, and that was that. By the time Jams and Skyler had left for flight school two weeks later, Roy and Helen had been happy to consider Skyler a part of their family.

Unfortunately, that also meant that she was held to their moral standards, just as they held their son to those standards, and sleeping around was not okay in their book.

Jams rubbed the bridge of his nose, a habit he'd picked up from Skyler when he was hesitant at answering a question.

"Oh, Helen, calm down," Roy said to his wife, saving Jams from having to answer. "Skyler is having a rough time, and that's what some people do when they don't deal with things properly. They look for ways to escape what they're feeling. "

Helen made a disgusted sound in the back of her throat, but didn't reply.

Jams and his father exchanged a grin.

"Well, you know how I feel," Roy said to his son. "She's your responsibility so you take care of her, any way you have to."

Jams nodded, remembering their conversation two and a half years earlier. After the crash in Iraq, both Jams and Skyler had gone home to his parents' farm to recover. Skyler had spent hours every day riding one of their horses over the far and wide ranges. The devasta-

50

tion she felt had been crystal clear in every movement she made. It had been then that Roy had told Jams that she was his partner, and therefore it was his responsibility to look after her.

"You make sure she gets through this," Roy had told him. "She needs you son. She may not show you that 'cause she's every bit as hardheaded as any man I've ever known, but she needs you more than she probably knows. You be there for her." It was an order, and Jams took it to heart.

Skyler and Devin arrived at the restaurant shortly after Jams and his parents were seated. Skyler held Devin's hand, leading her to the table. Roy and Jams immediately stood, Devin grinned at the old-fashioned, but gallant courtesy.

"Mom, Dad," Skyler said smiling proudly. "This is Devin."

Devin smiled at the couple, extending her hand to Roy and smiling at Helen. "It's really nice to meet you."

Roy took her hand giving it a gentle squeeze as he smiled. He looked her over; she wasn't what he'd expected at all. She was definitely a beautiful girl, but he was surprised by the purple in her black hair and all the earrings in her ears and the one in her eyebrow. She looked like a punk rock girl, but then she wore very stylish looking clothes. She was definitely her own person, which was probably a good thing when paired with someone as vibrant as Skyler.

"It's lovely to meet you too," Roy smiled.

Devin turned, reaching her hand out to Helen, who clasped her hand in both of hers. "It's wonderful to meet you, Devin," Helen greeted her warmly.

Skyler caught the waitress that walked by and asked for a beer and a shot. "Anyone else want something? Babe?"

"No, I'm good," Devin said, smiling gently and knowing that Skyler was likely to drink a few tonight.

On the way to the restaurant "Angels Fall" had come on the car stereo again. Skyler had uttered the word "fuck" and reached over to turn it up. Devin had taken her hand immediately, holding it the entire time the song played, squeezing gently when she saw Skyler choke up on a few lines. They hadn't talked about it after it ended, but Skyler hadn't pulled her hand away this time either. Devin considered it progress.

"Beer," Jams said.

"Second that," Roy said, holding up a finger.

"I'll just have soda dear," Helen said.

Skyler gave the waitress the order smiling at her. Devin looked on, noticing the mild flirt that occurred. Skyler had that way with people, especially women. It never went anywhere and Devin seriously doubted if Skyler even realized she did it.

When they were all seated again, and the drinks came, Skyler threw back the shot and chased it with half a bottle of beer. Jams eyed her, and Skyler caught the look.

"Damned Breaking Benjamin and their song," Skyler said by way of explanation.

"Aw," Jams said, tilted his beer bottle to hers, and they clinked them together. "Angels Fall."

Devin looked at Jams' parents to see how they reacted to the display. Roy looked appropriately respectful, and Helen nodded her head sadly. So apparently they knew about the crash and the relevance of the song. She looked at Skyler, wanting to ask. Skyler caught the look, even as she held up a finger to the waitress, Jams doing the same.

"I can feel the question… go ahead," Skyler said.

"The song?" Devin asked.

Jams nodded, giving Skyler a look that said "tell her." Skyler nodded too, as if receiving the message telepathically.

"Billy Kings," Skyler said, her eyes taking a slightly haunted look. "We called him Benny, because he had an obsession with the band Breaking Benjamin."

"We had to hear every new song they put out," Jams said, rolling his eyes with a sad grin.

"It was on regular rotation in the copter," Skyler said. Her eyes connected with Jams', and they both smiled, thinking of how many times they'd heard every song and how Benny sang along with every single one.

Devin nodded, happy to finally be hearing at least part of the story. She noticed that Roy and Helen both had tears in their eyes, so she guessed that they had met Benny a few times.

"The song "Angels Fall" came out after the crash," Jams said, his eyes on Skyler.

Devin saw Skyler close her eyes slowly, pressing her lips together. They'd listened to it together when they'd gotten the new album, in honor of Benny.

"It was like he'd had them write it and send it to us," Skyler said, her voice shaky with unshed tears.

Devin felt tears sting the back of her eyes. She nodded, now fully understanding why Skyler couldn't turn it off when it came on. It was like Benny speaking to her from the grave, and she couldn't just shut him off.

"And you were 'angels.' " Devin confirmed.

"We used to call ourselves Hells Angels," Jams said.

Thinking of the sadness in the song lyrics made Devin feel an overwhelming sorrow. She easily sensed that this was just the tip of the iceberg of the tragedy..

"Maybe I'll have one too," Devin said as the waitress brought Skyler's second shot.

"A round for the table," Roy said.

When the drinks arrived a few moments later, Roy stood and lifted his glass. "To Billy and Tommy."

"Angles Fall," Skyler and Jams said, standing and raising their glasses. Devin and even Helen stood too, toasting.

They sat, taking a few minutes to look at the menus and collect themselves.

After a minute or two, Devin reached a hand over to Skyler, leaning close to her. "Thank you," she whispered.

Skyler looked at her for a long moment, realizing how hard it must be for Devin to not know everything, and only get crumbs at a time. She instantly regretted that she wasn't able to talk about the rest of it, but she knew she was going to have nightmares just from talking about it this much.

Skyler squeezed Devin's hand gently, smiling at her, even while her eyes were still haunted by the fresh memory.

After everyone ordered, Roy and Helen focused on getting to know Devin.

"So Skyler says you work with computers?" Roy queried.

Devin smiled, nodding. "Yes, with computer language mostly."

"What's computer language?" Helen asked.

"Basically, it's the code behind a program. It's a series of commands and information to run a program."

"And what do you do with this code?" Roy asked, looking a little perplexed.

"Well, sometimes I'm looking for viruses."

"Viruses?" Helen asked.

"Basically code that someone has put into a program to make it do what they want it to do. For instance, someone might upload a virus to a bank program to make it download all of someone's money into their own account."

"So you stop people from stealing other people's money?" Roy clarified.

"Sometimes. Right now I'm working with the police department to break up a ring of identity thieves."

"Identity thieves?" Helen queried, sounding like she was trying to speak a foreign language.

"It's when someone uses other people's information, their social security number, name, birth date, stuff like that, to apply for credit cards or loans. They never pay for what they get, and it ruins the credit of the person whose identity was stolen."

"Wow," Roy said nodding, "sounds impressive."

"Well, they've been trying to get this particular group for about two years now. They finally called me in about a month ago."

"Well, if you're able to catch these people, why didn't they call you sooner?" Helen asked.

"Uh…" Devin said, grimacing as she glanced at Skyler.

"Because they had to figure out if they could afford her, Mom." Skyler said.

Roy and Helen looked over at Devin, and she nodded confirming what Skyler had said.

"You charge that much?" Roy asked.

Devin bit her lip, feeling uncomfortable.

"Dad, she has a PhD from MIT," Skyler put in. "Her student loan payments are probably more than my apartment payment!"

Devin chuckled, dropping her head. "They probably aren't quite that much, but they're not cheap."

"Besides," Skyler said, "Devin's one of the best at this."

Roy and Helen nodded, impressed by the degree that Devin held, as well as the fact that Skyler was defending her.

"Well, it does sound like you do really important things with that degree of yours," Roy said, looking at Helen. "Imagine, our Skyler is dating a doctor."

Skyler looked over at Jams. "That's my girl," she said, nodding her head toward Devin.

"Blah, blah, blah," Jams said, rolling his eyes.

"What's your girl do?" Skyler asked, her eyes dancing.

"Shut up," Jams said, his eyes narrowed.

"You're dating someone?" Helen asked her son, surprised.

"I hate you," Jams said to Skyler, and turned to his mother. "Not really Mom, she's just kind of casual right now, and not anyone I'd want you to meet yet."

Skyler leaned back in her chair, picking up her beer as she winked at Devin. Devin grinned, knowing that this was probably something she and Jams did often. They really were like brother and sister. It was an interesting evening.

Chapter 3

A few weeks after dinner with Jams' parents, Skyler was driving Devin to work. Devin's Hummer was in the shop for maintenance and Skyler had offered to drive her in. Skyler was almost always at Devin's house now, even though it was a much longer commute than from her apartment.

Skyler's phone rang a few minutes into the drive, she glanced at the display, rolled her eyes, but answered the call on the hands free, glancing at Devin as she did.

"Yeah?" Skyler said as she answered the phone.

"Skyla?" came a clipped reply, the voice was male, and had a distinct accent.

"Hey Dad," Skyler replied, sounding highly unenthusiastic. "What's up?"

"When you comin' home girl?" the man asked.

Skyler took a deep breath, blowing it out slowly as she shook her head. "I told you, Dad, I can't get home any time soon."

"What about Sebo? He needs ya," the man replied, his accent definitely Cajun.

Devin found herself wondering what Skyler's parents were like. She listened to the conversation with fascination.

"He got hisself into trouble," Skyler snapped, "he can get hisself out." Her accent was a clear as day at that point.

The man made a disgusted sound at the other end of the line. Skyler just waited, her index finger tapping agitatedly on the steering wheel.

"I dun understand you," the man said, his tone vexed. "Yer brutha needs ya girl."

Skyler narrowed her eyes, retorting. "What he needs is ta stop sellin' drugs."

Once again the man made a grunt of disgust, "Dun undastand ya," he said again.

"Oh, I know that," Skyler said, rolling her eyes and glancing at Devin.

"Heas ya ma," her father said then, as he apparently handed the phone over to someone else.

"What's dis?" came a woman's voice. "You not comin' home?"

Skyler curled her lip in obvious irritation. "No, ma, I'm not comin' home. I told you that. I got a busy season comin' up and we gotta get prepared."

"Busy season?" the woman repeated, her tone incredulous. "More impor'ant dan family?"

Skyler actually laughed out loud at that question. "Yeah, ma, savin' lives is more impor'ant than family."

"What da hell is wrong which ya?" the woman snapped. "Yer brotha he needs ya righ' now."

"What he needs is a lawyer, ma," Skyler said, her tone indicating her annoyance. "Maybe you should call one a dem."

The woman gasped in shock.

"Look, I gotta go," Skyler said, apparently taking advantage of the shocked silence that followed the gasp. Before the woman could even reply, Skyler ended the call.

"I'm guessing those were your parents."

"Uh-huh," Skyler confirmed.

"Are all of your conversations with them that acrimonious?"

Skyler couldn't help but grin at the word Devin used, she definitely sounded every bit the educated woman she was at times.

"Lately, yes," Skyler said.

"Why lately? And who is Sebo?"

"Well, we've never had a good relationship," Skyler said, "but lately they've been hounding me to come home because of Sebo. Sebo, his real name is Sebastian, is my brother. He's in trouble and they want me to help."

"Law enforcement trouble?"

"Yep."

"For selling drugs?"

"Yep," Skyler confirmed.

"Why do they think you can help him? They do know you're not a cop, right?"

"Oh, they know," Skyler said. "They just think I can use my influence to get him released."

Devin looked over at her. "No offense," she said, "but what influence do they think you have that would help in this situation?"

Skyler hesitated, and that's what cued Devin in that it was something she didn't necessarily want to talk about. Which was why Devin was surprised when Skyler made the next comment.

"They think a Medal of Honor will get you anywhere."

Her tone was so blasé that Devin didn't catch the significance of what she'd just said until she replayed it in her head.

"Wait," Devin said, putting her hand on Skyler's arm, "you have a Medal of Honor?"

Skyler's lips twitched, but she nodded.

"Isn't that kind of a big deal?"

Skyler shrugged non-committedly.

"As in the President of the United States presents it to you?" Devin said, her tone incredulous at Skyler's attitude.

Skyler glanced over at Devin, her look unreadable. "It's in my sock drawer at the apartment," she said, her tone indicating that it couldn't be that big of a deal if it was there.

"That doesn't make it less important, Skyler," Devin said, narrowing her eyes at the other woman. "Did you get it because of the crash?" she asked, thinking it had something to do with the subject Skyler didn't talk about.

"I got a Purple Heart for that. This was something else."

"But you don't want talk about it, do you?"

Skyler looked over at Devin, realizing that Devin was quickly learning to read her cues. It was kind of shock to her, no woman had gotten close enough to do that in a long time.

"Not much to talk about… group of insurgents, they're dead, I'm not."

Devin looked back at her for a few long minutes, knowing there was more to it than that, but not wanting to push.

"Okay then," Devin said, with a smile. "So you don't believe they want to see you when they're asking you to come home?"

Skyler looked over at Devin for a moment, her look saying pretty much everything, but she said, "Did you hear them ask me how I was doing?"

"No."

"Yeah, that's how I know they don't care about seeing me."

"When's the last time you went back home?"

"It's been awhile."

"Have you been home since you got back from Iraq?" Devin asked her tone softer.

Skyler heard the tone, and knew that Devin was being careful around the subject of Iraq and appreciated it.

"No," Skyler said, shaking her head.

"So it's really just that they want you to help Sebastian."

"Yep."

"I don't understand that, they should be proud of you, for all you've done, all you accomplished," Devin stated indignantly.

Skyler found herself grinning at the sound of it, Jams was usually her biggest cheerleader.

"Well, they think the sun shines out of Sebo's ass, so…"

"Hmph!" Devin huffed.

Skyler laughed at the sound.

"Okay, okay, easy now," Skyler said, smiling.

Devin grinned at Skyler's words. It was nice being able to ask some questions of Skyler. She knew there were some things that she couldn't ask about, but she liked that Skyler was being a little more open to answering questions about herself these days.

The following week, Skyler and her crew became extremely busy with wildfires that began in the Angeles National Forest near the San Gabriel Mountains. Skyler couldn't make it back to the house in Malibu at all, as they worked long shifts and half the time slept in the hangar when they were off shift.

One evening, the crew got a night off; Skyler had texted Devin as she got ready to leave the hangar. By the time Devin got to Skyler's apartment two hours later, Skyler had already showered and was lying in bed dozing. Devin walked into the room, standing at the foot of the bed watching Skyler sleep. Skyler wore black sweatpants and a green Army tank top, one arm was thrown above her head casually.

Somehow Skyler sensed her there and opened her eyes.

"Hi," Devin said, smiling as she walked around to the side of the bed, moving to sit down next to where Skyler lay.

"Hey," Skyler replied, her voice scratchy.

"Oh, you sound terrible," Devin said, leaning down to kiss Skyler.

"You say the sweetest things."

Devin pulled back, looking down at Skyler, her eyes taking in the exhaustion Skyler was obviously feeling.

"Still didn't sleep much, huh?"

"Mmm," Skyler said, closing her eyes tiredly.

"Okay, you sleep," Devin said, softly. "I'll be here when you wake up."

With that, Devin kicked off her shoes and lay down next to Skyler. Skyler's arm immediately encircled her shoulders, pulling her closer. They lay that way for a long while, and when Devin was sure Skyler was deep asleep, she carefully moved to get up.

Walking through the apartment, Devin could hear Jams snoring in his room down the hall, opposite Skyler's room. The apartment had two master bedrooms; it was a very nice upscale place.

Devin poked around in the kitchen, trying to think of something to make the two pilots when they woke up. She was thinking of soup, having heard how hoarse Skyler was, probably from the all the smoke.

Eventually she settled on chicken soup and realized she'd need to run to the store for some of the ingredients. She left and returned an hour later, happily noting that Skyler was still asleep.

It was another three hours before Jams appeared in the kitchen.

"What is that smell?" he asked.

Devin glanced over her shoulder at him. "It's called home cooked food, you might have heard of it."

Jams looked like he was trying to remember, then shook his head. "Nope, MREs and take out, those are the only food groups I know."

"And I bet your mother would be ashamed of you," Devin chided.

Jams grinned widely, nodding, as he walked over to the pot boiling on the stove. Devin handed him a spoon and he sampled some of the soup.

"Oh..." he said, awestruck, "this is good this *home cooked food* that you speak of."

Devin chuckled. "Just wait, there's bread too."

Jams breathed a deep sigh. "If you weren't gay, I'd marry ya."

"You'd what?" came Skyler's voice from the other side of the kitchen.

Jams and Devin laughed. Skyler walked into the kitchen, leaned down to smell the soup and then leaned in to kiss Devin.

"Smells, great babe."

A little while later the three of them sat on the balcony of the apartment eating and talking. It was definitely getting chilly as Devin shivered. Skyler stood up, taking off her sweat jacket and put it around Devin's shoulders. Devin smiled at the gesture, and she gratefully put her arms into the sleeves.

"So, how is it going out there?" Devin asked, referring to the fires.

"'Bout seventy-five percent contained," Skyler said.

Jams nodded in agreement. "Yeah, maybe another couple of days, then we'll be good."

"Then you can go back to normal?" Devin asked.

"Yeah, saving people from cliff sides and shit," Jams said, grinning.

Devin canted her head, looking at the two. "Speaking of which, what did you two think of that movie San Andreas?"

Jams and Skyler looked at each other, then back at Devin.

"It was cute," Jams said.

"The daughter was hot," Skyler replied.

"Oh yeah," Jams said, "the mom was pretty hot too."

Devin laughed. "I mean the helicopter stuff."

"Oh," Skyler said, grinning, "yeah, that was all bullshit."

"All of it?" Devin asked incredulously.

"Well," Jams said, looking over at Skyler, "we do fly helicopters at LA Rescue."

"So, yeah, that wasn't bullshit," Skyler said.

"No 'tipping the hat'?" Devin asked, referencing a maneuver in the movie.

"Yeah," Skyler said slowly, "that was just stupid."

"You can't do that kind of thing?" Devin asked.

"No one can do that kind of thing," Jams said.

"Well, The Rock can, in a movie," Skyler said amiably.

"Yeah, true," Jams agreed.

"Oh and I loved how even when the blades hit the rock face, they stayed intact. That was awesome," Skyler said, grinning.

"Yeah, we need to get us some of those!" Jams agreed.

Devin watched the two go back and forth with an amused grin on her face, it was obviously something that had been discussed at length.

"And how come you don't go on back and help Tom and Jerry with the rescues?" Jams asked Skyler. "You know, like The Rock did in the movie. At least he helped his crew."

"Yeah, that was great, he's a nice guy," Skyler said. "I can't auto rotate down either, not like that."

"That's not something that's done either?" Devin asked weakly.

"Sure it is," Jams said.

"In the movies," Skyler said, smiling.

Devin laughed, shaking her head. "Okay, so not so realistic that movie, huh?"

"Not in the flying helicopters part, no," Skyler said. "Don't even get me started on what our maintenance chief would say to us if we brought a copter back in the condition he did. We'd be in the CO's office for an hour with our heads ripped off for good measure. Not to mention endangering the lives of the crew as well as that news team they had with them when they decided to showboat that fictional shit."

Devin nodded. "I can see that you didn't really like the movie."

"Oh, we liked the movie," Jams said.

"Gave us a little boost in popularity," Skyler said, grinning. "We just fly according to the laws of physics, in that movie they didn't."

"Aw," Devin said, nodding and wisely steering the conversation away from the movie. "So, nice weather we're having, huh?"

Jams and Skyler laughed at her quick change of topic.

"Enjoy it now," Jams said, holding up his bottle of beer to Skyler, she immediately clinked the bottom of hers to the bottom of his.

"Why do you say that?" Devin asked.

"With this El Niño thing they're predicting," Skyler said, seriously. "There's going to be a lot of rain, and that's going to mean a lot of work."

"With car accidents and stuff?" Devin asked.

"With everything, high surf, high winds, floods, fires, mudslides, you name it." Skyler said, looking resolved.

Devin nodded, not having realized that there'd be a busy season for a rescue team, but it did make sense.

Two months later, the rains began in earnest. Within two weeks, Skyler was exhausted and catching a cold. Devin came home one night to find Skyler lying on the couch in her living room.

"Hey," Devin said, walking around to look at Skyler's face, she immediately saw that Skyler felt awful.

"Hey," Skyler responded listlessly.

Devin heard the congestion immediately, and sat down on the couch, reaching her hand out to touch Skyler's face.

"Oh, babe, you're burning up."

Skyler sniffed, looking completely wiped out.

"Come on," Devin said, putting her bag aside and standing up.

"Where are we going?" Skyler asked sounding lifeless.

"We," Devin said, as she put her hand out to help Skyler up off the couch, "are going to get you into a nice hot steamy shower, and get you medicated so you can get some sleep." She stopped then, looking back at Skyler. "How long are you off?" she asked, realizing suddenly that Skyler may only be off a few hours.

"Chief gave us two days off."

"Good!" Devin said, then continued back down the hall and into the master bathroom.

An hour later, Devin had Skyler tucked into bed. She fed her chicken soup and made her some tea that would help ease her congestion. Before she'd even finished eating, Skyler was falling asleep.

Devin got her to lie down and made sure she was comfortable, then turned off lights. That night she lay next to Skyler, listening to her breathe, and feeling happy that Skyler was willing to let her take care of her when she was sick. Devin had been with strong women before who simply wanted to hide away when they were sick, or worse were complete jerks about it. Skyler just let Devin do her best to make her feel better.

When Skyler woke later that night, she lay listening to the rain on the roof, and glanced over at Devin sleeping next to her. Devin was turned on her side, her hand on Skyler's chest. Skyler reached up touching Devin's hand with hers. She reflected on how it felt to let someone take care of her. It felt good to be comfortable enough to let herself go and to let Devin see her during her weak moments. It wasn't something she was given to doing normally, but this little slip of a girl was winding her way into her heart through the smallest gestures. Skyler fell asleep with her hand still covering Devin's.

Devin woke the next morning, feeling the warmth of Skyler's hand on hers. Moving carefully to sit up, she reached for her phone. She texted the people she was working with at the police department to let them know she wouldn't be in for a couple of days. She fully intended to dedicate her time to helping Skyler feel better.

When Skyler woke later that morning, Devin made her breakfast and coaxed her to eat what she could. Skyler grinned at the mothering tone in Devin's voice when she told her to drink some orange juice because it was "good for her." At one point they went out to the living room where they sat and watched TV. When Skyler got sleepy, she lay down on the couch, with her head in Devin's lap. She fell asleep to the feel of Devin's hand stroking her hair.

At the end of her time off, Skyler was feeling moderately better, and she knew it was because Devin had made her rest and eat well. Before leaving on her first morning back, Skyler turned in the doorway, taking Devin in her arms as she did and kissed her deeply, then pulled back to look down into Devin's eyes.

"Thank you for taking care of me," Skyler said softly.

"Thank you for letting me take care of you."

Skyler kissed her again, and then turned to head to her car. Devin left the house a little while later, clouds were already gathering on the horizon.

The crew was thirteen hours into a fourteen hour shift and had just touched down and shut down the engines at Van Nuys Airport. Skyler was finishing her shut down procedures when her phone started ringing. Pulling out her phone, she saw that it was Devin. Tuning her phone to her headset so she could continue her checks, she answered the phone, thinking it was odd that Devin would call her while she knew she was on duty

"Hey, babe, what's up?" Skyler answered.

There was an eerie silence that sent a chill up Skyler's spine immediately. She put her hand up to alert Jams that there was something wrong.

"Devin?" Skyler asked, strongly. "Babe?"

There was heavy breathing, and Skyler felt her stomach plummet, as she heard the faintest whisper, "Skyler?"

"I'm here, babe, what's happening? Talk to me!" As she said it, she switched the comms over so that Jams could hear it in his headset.

"I'm… there's… Skyler?" Devin said, her voice tremulous.

"What's happened babe?" Skyler asked.

"I was… I was coming home…" Devin began, her voice halting and out of breath. "There was… something hit my car… I can't see out… Skyler I can't see!"

"Okay, babe, calm down, you gotta tell me where you are," Skyler said, her tone was calm but her hands shook.

Putting one arm up, Skyler made the motion for starting the rotors on the helicopter. Jams nodded and restarted the engines as he tried to listen to what was happening. Tom and Jerry, still in the main fuselage, buckled themselves back in, preparing to head out again. Skyler heard Jams on the radio, requesting a mission deviation. She also heard control giving him grief but she shook her head at him, there was no way they weren't going.

"I was going home…" Devin said, her voice small.

Skyler winced as she did her best to hear Devin over the sound of the rotors starting.

"Okay, were you on Highway 1?" Skyler asked, knowing the route to Devin's house.

"Yes… Skyler? I'm so scared… I don't know where I am… I don't know… there's glass everywhere…" Devin was crying now.

Skyler had to control herself, knowing that if she lost it, she was going to be no good to Devin.

"Babe, stay with me," Skyler said, as she motioned for takeoff. "What was the last landmark you remember seeing?"

"What?" Devin asked, still crying.

"What did you see babe? What was near you? What's the last thing you remember?"

"I... I remember that Japanese place... Um... Nobu... I saw that..." Devin said, sounding calmer as she had something else to focus on.

"Good, babe, that's really good," Skyler said, motioning for Jams to pull the restaurant up on the navigation. "Okay, how long do you think it was before you got hit, after you saw Nobu? Five minutes? Ten?"

"Um... five," Devin said.

"Great, that's perfect babe, we're coming for you, okay? I'll be there, I promise," Skyler said, infusing her voice with confidence.

"Okay..." Devin said, sniffling.

"Do you know what hit you?" Skyler asked then, turning the aircraft west to head towards Highway 1, as Jams calculated the distance.

"I think it was mud..." Devin said, sounding scared again.

"Stay calm babe," Skyler told her, "I'm coming for you right now. Are you hurt?"

There was silence for a few moments, and Skyler wondered if Devin had passed out.

"My head hurts..." Devin said, "and my arm... I don't know... what else."

"That's okay, babe, that's okay. Are you bleeding?" Skyler asked, as Jams motioned to her. He showed her the points on the navigation screen, she nodded, making corrections to their flight path. Putting her hand over the mike she said, "Call it in, there's probably going to be more cars hit."

"Roger that," Jams said nodding as he got on the radio.

"Devin?" Skyler asked when she realized Devin hadn't answered her.

There was silence for a long time. Skyler pushed the stick forward, pushing the engines in her need to get to Devin quicker.

"Easy…" Jams cautioned, then turned his head to look behind him. "You two get ready, we're gonna need to get in there fast, no telling how precarious this vehicle's gonna be," he said, wincing as he realized he was talking about Skyler's girlfriend. He glanced at his partner; she only shook her head in response, basically telling him she couldn't think about that.

"What's our fuel look like?" Skyler asked, knowing they hadn't been too low when they'd landed.

"We got about sixty minutes to bingo," Jams told her.

Skyler nodded doing the calculations in her head and knowing they were going to be cutting it close if they really had to look for Devin's vehicle. Fortunately, Devin drove a massive white Hummer, it should be hard to miss. Skyler prayed it would be hard to miss.

"Devin, you still with me?" Skyler asked.

"Yes," Devin answered, but her voice was very faint.

"I'll be there in five minutes, you hold on, okay?" Skyler said.

"Okay," Devin said weakly.

It was the longest five minute flight of Skyler's life, and she pushed the helicopter to its full 122 knot capability, knowing she was pushing it, but she couldn't lose this particular race. She knew that the mudslide could have pushed Devin over the cliffs at Malibu, but she also knew that just because it hadn't yet, didn't mean it couldn't at any moment. Time was of the essence.

"We're nearing the coordinates," Jams said, looking at the instruments.

"Roger that," Skyler responded, slipping into full rescue mode and doing her best to forget that this time they were rescuing someone who was extremely important to her.

"Come left fifteen," Jams said.

"Do you have anything?" Skyler called to the guys in the back.

"Nothing yet," Jerry called, "searching!"

"Come left another five," Jams said.

"Roger that," Skyler confirmed.

"Anything?!" Jams called.

"White SUV! Got it!" Tom yelled triumphantly.

"Take her down," Jams said.

"Roger, taking her down," Skyler said, nodding. "Devin?" she tried again.

"I hear you!" Devin called, tears in her voice.

"I'm here babe," Skyler said, "just sit tight. Jerry's coming to get you."

"Okay," Devin replied, sounding childlike suddenly.

It took thirty minutes to get Jerry down to the SUV, and for him to get through the sunroof, into the vehicle and get Devin in the basket. Skyler was fairly certain she held her breath the entire time.

"I've got her!" Jerry finally called.

"Bringing them up!" Tom called.

"Holding steady," Skyler replied. "Where we at on fuel?"

"Twenty-five to bingo, we're cutting it close," Jams warned.

"Roger that, twenty-five to bingo, and I'm pushing it," Skyler said, adding the last with a grin.

"Roger that," Jams replied grinning with relief.

"Rescue on board!" Tom called from the back of the aircraft.

"How is she?" Skyler called, wishing she could see Devin at that moment.

"She's banged up, and her pulse is all over the place. She's lost some blood, we need to get her back now."

"Roger that," Jams said, when he saw Skyler pale slightly.

"Radio ahead," Skyler said, her voice not quite as strong suddenly.

"Stay with me partner," Jams said, his tone strong.

Skyler nodded, blowing out her breath and refocusing.

"Control this is Rescue ten," Jams said into the mike. "We've got an injured woman, age twenty-seven to twenty-nine, height five foot four, approximately one hundred twenty-five pounds. She has a head injury and possible internal injuries. We're getting a weak pulse, request ambulance on scene when we land."

Skyler listened to Jams making the radio call, and took that time to collect herself. When he glanced over at her as he closed his mike he saw that she was back in control of herself. They made the flight back and even had a couple of minutes of fuel left to spare. They all knew that they would likely get reamed for ignoring mission control when they refused to deviate their mission, but if Devin was okay, it was worth it. Skyler didn't even want to think about how close the Hummer had been to the edge of the cliff.

Skyler rode in the ambulance with Devin, holding her hand the entire time, even though Devin had passed out before they'd set the helicopter down at the airport. At the hospital, Skyler paced waiting to hear from the doctor. The hospital had gotten contact information from the LAPD for Devin's parents and had called them. Skyler felt stupid not having any of that information.

An hour after getting to the hospital, the doctor walked out, just as Jams joined Skyler in the waiting area. Devin's parents hadn't arrived yet.

"For Devin James?" the doctor queried.

Skyler stepped up to the doctor.

"How is she?" she asked worried.

"Are you a family member?" the doctor asked.

Skyler looked back at the man for a minute, wanting to punch him for asking her such a stupid question.

"She's the pilot that rescued her," Jams put in, his tone serious.

The doctor looked at the two of them; they were both wearing their flight suits with the LA Fire Department Air Operations patches on them.

"She's also my girlfriend," Skyler put in for good measure.

The doctor looked like he wanted to debate the point. Fortunately, Devin's parents walked up at that moment.

"We're Devin's parents," said the woman walking up to the doctor, "and anything you have to share with us, can be shared with the people that saved her life."

Skyler glanced over at the woman, she was definitely no nonsense; she liked that.

The doctor nodded. "Ms. James has suffered a minor head injury with some scalp lacerations. She's got some abrasions and contusions, but all in all she's in good condition. We'll want to keep her for a couple of days to make sure the head injury isn't something we should be more concerned about. "

"Thank you, doctor," said Devin's mother. "When can we see her?"

"You can see the nurse at the desk; she'll take you to see her," the doctor told them.

The doctor turned and walked away then. Skyler turned to Devin's mother, extending her hand. "I'm Skyler," she said, smiling at the other woman.

"It's good to meet you Skyler," Devin's mother said, shaking her hand. "I'm Suzanne and that's Harold. Thank you so much for rescuing our daughter."

"Yes," agreed Devin's father, a tall man with black hair, and brown eyes, "thank you."

Skyler nodded, not sure if they'd heard what she'd said about dating Devin. She looked at Suzanne, and saw where Devin got her petite size, and her eyes; her eyes were the same rich emerald green as Devin's, but Suzanne's hair was red. Devin's dad was definitely where Devin had gotten her dark hair, but she didn't have very many other features from her father. He seemed quite happy to let Suzanne do all the talking.

"Let's go see our girl, shall we?" Suzanne said to the group.

Suzanne led the way to the nurses station. The nurse tried to say that Skyler and Jams couldn't visit Devin because they weren't family, that didn't work with Suzanne.

"I'm her mother, and I'm saying they can see my daughter," she pronounced and proceeded down the hall.

Skyler and Jams grinned at each other, and followed along.

The room they entered was dimly lit, Devin lay on the bed, a bandage on her head. Skyler had to hold herself back from walking straight over to her; she didn't want to push her luck with Devin's parents. That went out the window when Devin opened her eyes at their entry and looked straight at Skyler.

"Sky?" Devin said softly.

Skyler strode over to the side of the bed, reaching her hand down to very gently touch the bruise on Devin's cheek.

"You scared me to death," Skyler told her honestly.

Devin looked back at her for a long moment, tears in her eyes. "And you saved my life."

Skyler smiled. "What else was I gonna do?"

"How fired are you?" Even though Devin smiled, she was concerned.

"You don't worry about that."

"But Sky," Devin began. Skyler's finger on her lips stopped her.

"I'll take whatever they throw at me, but there was no way I wasn't coming for you. If they can't understand that, I can't work for them."

Devin blinked a couple of times, looking very affected by what Skyler was saying, but only nodding in response. Her eyes moved to her parents then and Skyler stepped back, but Devin held her hand out to her. Skyler took Devin's hand, and moved to sit in the chair next to the bed. Devin squeezed her hand, Skyler squeezed gently back. Skyler suddenly realized that Devin's parents made Devin nervous.

"Hi there, honey," Suzanne said, stepping forward and leaning down to kiss her daughter's cheek.

"Hi Mom," Devin said, sounding very young.

"You banged yourself up pretty good, huh?" Harold said, moving in to kiss her cheek as well.

"Yeah," Devin said softly.

"We understand that your connections came in handy in this case," Suzanne said, looking over at Skyler and smiling.

Devin glanced back at Skyler. "Yeah, it's pretty handy to know a rescue pilot when you're trapped in a mudslide at the edge of a cliff."

"Indeed!" Harold said.

"Did you guys meet Jams?" Devin asked then, noticing him hovering in the back.

"No," Suzanne said, turning to look at Jams suddenly, "Jams?"

"It's actually Daniel. Jams is my call sign."

"Call sign?" Suzanne queried.

"It's a pilot thing, Mom," Devin said, winking at Jams.

"So you're a pilot?" Harold asked, looking interested.

"I'm Sky's copilot," Jams said, nodding toward Skyler.

Harold nodded, looking impressed with both of them.

Devin's parents stayed for a little while longer, but then said they'd come back the next day, they didn't want to tire her. Jams also excused himself, telling Skyler he was going to go check in with their CO and see when their next shift was scheduled.

"You lay there and get better," Jams told Devin, winking at her.

"Yes sir."

When they were alone Skyler moved the chair closer to Devin's bed, putting her on eye level with the girl.

"You should be home getting some sleep," Devin said after a long moment of looking Skyler's face over.

"I'm not leaving."

"Sky…" Devin began, but Skyler shook her head.

They had a staring match, which Skyler won, because Devin was getting tired again.

"Fine. Then come lie here with me," she said, patting the side of the bed.

"I don't think the hospital will appreciate that. I'm fine, babe, I can sleep right here."

"No, you can't. You're not going to get good sleep that way."

"I'm fine."

"You're going to get over here, or I'm going to…"

"Going to what?" Skyler countered.

"Meanie," Devin said, pouting prettily.

"Oh, sure, pull out the big guns," Skyler said, rolling her eyes. "Okay, okay, you win."

Skyler bent down, unlacing her boots and kicking them off. Then she got up and walked around to the other side of the bed, climbed in carefully. Fortunately, Devin wasn't on an IV, so there were no tubes or wires to avoid. Lying on her side, Skyler slid her arm under Devin's neck carefully, and rested her other hand lightly on Devin's stomach.

"Is this okay?" Skyler asked.

Devin responded by snuggling closer to Skyler, putting her hand on Skyler's hand that rested on her stomach.

Skyler smiled fondly, thinking this night could have turned out so differently and ever grateful that it hadn't. Within minutes the two of them were asleep. When the first nurse came in to check Devin's vitals she stopped and looked at the two. The story of what had happened with these two had made it around to all the staff in the hospital, and seeing them lying together warmed the nurse's heart.

Skyler's eyes opened when she felt the nurse reach for Devin's hand to check her pulse.

"You're okay, honey," the nurse told her, when Skyler looked like she was going to move. "You had a rough night," the nurse said with a wink. "You just stay right there."

Skyler smiled at her, nodding tiredly, as she lowered her head, nuzzling it against Devin's head. The nurse left a minute later, smiling with tears in her eyes. She loved stories like these; it was rare, but she knew love when she saw it.

Devin woke first the next morning, when another nurse came to check her vitals. As the nurse walked out, Devin saw a woman standing in the doorway. She recognized the dark haired woman immediately and tensed automatically, which alerted Skyler, who stirred immediately.

"Damnit," Devin muttered, having not wanted to wake Skyler.

Sarah took in the scene before her, her brown eyes scanning the woman lying next to Devin on the hospital bed. She noted the flight suit the woman wore, twitching her lips in agitation. This was unexpected.

"What are you doing here?" Devin asked, her tone cool.

Skyler moved to sit up, looking down at Devin, and then followed the direction of her look and saw the woman in the doorway. She wore a Marine battle dress uniform, the name "Blankenship" on the patch. Skyler also noticed the possessive way she was looking at Devin, and that put her on alert immediately. Moving to get up, Skyler walked around the bed and sat in the chair she'd vacated the night before. She bent down to pull on her boots, glancing up at the woman who hadn't spoken yet.

Devin waited, looking at Sarah, her eyes then moving to Skyler who was lacing up her boots.

"I asked you a question," Devin said, sharply, which had Skyler standing up, and stepping closer to Devin.

Sarah moved into the room, her eyes connecting with Skyler's, reading a challenge in them. She narrowed her eyes at the woman, then looked at Devin again.

"I saw what happened," Sarah said, concerned.

Sarah saw Skyler tense as she stepped closer to Devin, which made her feel the need to reach out and touch Devin's hand. Devin moved it away immediately.

"Okay," Devin said, her tone unrelenting.

"Devin," Sarah said, beseeching, "don't be like that. I just got back a few days ago. I was going to call you."

"Why?"

Sarah narrowed her eyes at Devin, purposefully ignoring Skyler's presence. "Because I wanted to talk to you."

Skyler stood watching the exchange, knowing the other woman was trying to irritate her by ignoring her. Since Skyler had no idea who the other woman was, she didn't plan on interfering unless Devin looked like she needed her to.

"Are you okay?" Sarah asked when silence ensued for too long.

"Thanks to Sky," Devin said, glancing up at Skyler.

Skyler grinned down at her, knowing that Devin was purposely bringing her into the discussion.

Sarah's eyes shifted to Skyler and she gave her a nod of acknowledgement, then looked back at Devin.

"I'll call you next week," Sarah said confidently, accompanied with a jaunty wink. Then she pivoted on her heel and walked out of the room.

Fuckin' Marines, Skyler thought to herself, even as she rolled her eyes at the dramatic exit.

"I'm sorry," Devin said to her.

"For what," Skyler said, as she moved to sit on the edge of the bed.

Devin narrowed her eyes at Skyler, but didn't respond. A moment Later Jams appeared in the doorway.

"Sky," he said.

"Yo?" Skyler replied, moving to stand.

"We gotta go," Jams said, waving at Devin.

Skyler nodded, then leaned down to kiss Devin on the lips. "I'll be back when our shift is over."

"Fly safe," Devin said, reaching up to pull Skyler back for another kiss.

"You got it," Skyler grinned.

Chapter 4

Devin was released from the hospital the next day. Skyler was there to take her home and get her settled in the bedroom. After getting her lunch and her pain meds, Skyler sat with Devin, watching TV until she saw that Devin was getting tired. The doctors insisted that she rest as much as possible over the next few days. Once Devin was asleep, Skyler grabbed a beer from the fridge and walked out into Devin's backyard. Sitting down in one of the chairs, she pulled a cigarette out of her pack and pulled out her lighter.

She was still sitting out there twenty minutes later when Jams came around the side of the house, having hopped the fence when no one answered his light knock on the front door.

"Hey," he said, as he walked out.

Skyler glanced over her shoulder, nodding to her partner. "Hey, you let yourself in?"

"Yeah," Jams answered with a grin, "So she's home and settled?"

"Yep," Skyler said, nodding and blowing out a long stream of smoke.

Jams sat down across from his partner, looking at her, he could see that she was a bit agitated, since her knee was bouncing. He knew Skyler's signals, he'd learned them over the last fifteen years.

"So that was pretty damned close," he said, as he leaned back in the chair.

Skyler nodded, taking a long draw on her cigarette. "Yeah, too fucking close."

"Think she has any idea how close to the edge she really was?" Jams asked, raising an eyebrow.

"No," Skyler said, shaking her head, "and no one's going to tell her that either."

"No ma'am," he responded, grinning. "So who the fuck was that Marine the other day?"

Skyler grinned at the tone in Jams' voice, Army and Navy Marines didn't usually get along.

"Don't know for sure," Skyler said, rubbing her thumb over her bottom lip in agitation. "But I'm betting an ex."

"Aw," Jams said nodding, dropping his head to his chest, then he lifted his eyes to Skyler quizzically, "so what ya gonna do about that?"

Skyler looked back at him for a long moment, considering. She took the time to take another drag off her cigarette before she answered. "I'll take care of it."

"You better, you can't afford to let this one go."

"What makes you say that?"

"I'm not blind, Sky, I saw the panic on your face when she called you," he said, giving her a look that said she should know better.

Skyler nodded. "Yeah, I gotta say, I haven't been that scared in a long time."

Jams nodded, knowing exactly when she was that scared last. "So you make sure that whatever you do about that Marine sticks."

Skyler nodded, understanding his meaning.

Later that night, after they'd had dinner, they were relaxing on the couch. Devin was lying in front of Skyler, leaning back against Skyler's chest, her legs extended on the chaise portion of the sectional. Skyler's arms were around Devin's shoulders. Devin's phone rang. She picked it up, looking at the name on the display; Skyler saw that it said "Sarah" on it, with Sarah's picture. Devin hit ignore and set the phone down.

"So do you want to tell me who she is?" Skyler asked, casually.

Devin moved to sit up, turning to look at Skyler, her eyes searching Skyler's face. Skyler wondered if she was looking to see if there was any jealousy or anger. She wasn't sure what Devin was looking for, but Skyler intended to be careful with this conversation.

"She's an ex," Skyler stated.

"Yes."

Skyler nodded, waiting for the rest.

"She was in the Marines, and basically, even though DADT had been abolished, she wasn't out, and she wasn't planning on coming out."

Skyler nodded, she'd heard of a lot of gays that were still hesitant about coming out. "It happens a lot in the military."

"Right, but she wasn't out anywhere, her parents don't even know."

Skyler looked surprised, but nodded. She already knew that something like that wouldn't sit well with someone like Devin. She lived her life out loud, and anyone who didn't like it, could just deal with it.

"Okay…" Skyler said, knowing there was more.

"She got orders for Europe," Devin said, remembering that day with a distant look.

Skyler waited, not wanting to push. Devin's eyes settled back on hers again after a few moments.

"She wanted me to go with her," Devin said, her face a mask of derision, "but what was I going to do? Be the *friend* of hers?" She said the word "friend" like it was a curse word. In the gay community being referred to as someone's "friend" when you were actually dating the person, was a definite insult.

Skyler nodded, taking a deep breath and blowing it out. "That sucks."

"Yeah, it did, I was so in love with her, it wasn't even funny."

Skyler's chin came up at that admission, but she did her best not to overreact. Devin saw it instantly.

"Oh, Sky," she said, grimacing. "I'm sorry, I just meant that…"

"It's okay, I want you to tell me the truth here."

"I am," Devin assured her, placing her hand on Skyler's cheek and looking her in the eye.

Skyler nodded accepting that. "So what do you think she wants now?"

"Oh, I know what she wants."

"And that is?"

"She wants to tell me that she's out now."

"And you know this how?" Skyler asked, confused.

"She's not the only Marine I know that's stationed in Europe," Devin said, her eyes sparkling mischievously.

"Okay, and when she tells you she wants you back?" She wasn't sure where this was heading.

Devin looked back at her for a long moment. "That's the thing," Devin said, putting her arms around Skyler's neck. "I need to know where your head is right now."

"With us?"

"Yeah."

Skyler nodded, looking like she was gathering her thoughts. Then she looked Devin square in the eyes. "Almost losing you scared me to death, Devin. Not knowing if I'd get to you in time, or if that pile of mud would shift and send you over the edge… it scared me."

Devin nodded, not saying anything to interrupt Skyler's words.

"It made me realize that I love you," Skyler said so simply that Devin wasn't sure if she'd heard her right.

"Can you repeat that last part?" she asked, a smile starting on her lips.

Skyler slid her hands into Devin's hair, pulling her in to kiss her deeply, then pulling back to look into her eyes. "I love you."

The smile on Devin's face was so brilliant Skyler felt bad that she hadn't realized it sooner. She leaned in kissing Skyler back, her hands in Skyler's hair.

"So," Devin said, sitting back, "in answer to your question, when Sarah tells me she wants me back, I'm going to tell her that I'm in love with this pilot I'm dating."

"You are?"

"Oh yes, I think I have been since the moment I saw you."

"Interesting…" Skyler said, leaning in to kiss her again.

Devin and Skyler both returned to work by the end of the week. Devin was suffering no ill effects from her accident, she felt very lucky. Two other people had been killed in the same mudslide when their car had gone over the edge of the cliff. It was something that Devin thought about a lot; how lucky she'd been that Skyler and her crew had saved her. She'd found out that her Hummer had gone over the cliff approximately an hour after she'd been pulled out.

At the LAPD, she was hailed as the luckiest person alive.

"Guess it pays to date a rescue pilot, huh?" one of the guys asked, giving her a wink.

"It sure did this time," Devin said, smiling as she headed toward her temporary office.

Getting to the doorway of the office, she saw the plethora of lucky charms in her office. She saw rabbits' feet, four leaf clovers, even a box or two of Lucky Charms cereal. She turned around and saw that a lot of the people she was working with were standing around to see her reaction.

"Very funny…" she said, giving them all dirty looks, but her grin spoiling the effect.

Everyone got a good laugh that morning. When Devin told Skyler about it, she had a pretty good laugh as well.

"That's the danger of working with cops or firemen," Skyler said. "They're all jokers."

"Tell me about it!" Devin said laughing.

Later that day Devin got the call she was expecting from Sarah, she did her best to just decline the offer of lunch, but Sarah wouldn't give up. Devin finally relented and said she'd meet her for coffee that afternoon.

At four that afternoon, Devin walked into the Starbucks where they'd arranged to meet. Glancing around, she spotted Sarah easily as she was wearing her Marine fatigues. As she approached the table, Sarah stood up, leaning over to hug her. Devin allowed the hug, but turned her head when Sarah moved to kiss her.

Sarah noted the rebuff, but didn't comment. She hadn't come there to fight with Devin, far from it.

"Thanks for meeting me," Sarah said, smiling warmly. "I know you're busy."

Devin nodded. "Yeah, playing catch up for being out last week."

"How are you feeling?" Sarah asked, every bit the concerned ex.

"I'm fine," Devin said, recognizing Sarah's motives. "So, what do you want?"

"Wow," Sarah said, acting offended, "we can't just get together and talk?"

Devin just looked back at Sarah pausing, then she nodded slowly. "Yeah, we could, but that's not what this is about."

"What do you think this is about?" Sarah asked, acting as if there was no way Devin knew what she was talking about.

Again, Devin just sat looking back at the woman that she'd dated for three years, wondering how she'd never noticed how conniving and contrived Sarah was. Skyler wasn't exactly an open book, but Devin also knew there were very good reasons for her silence on certain things. Sarah, on the other hand, had no combat experience whatsoever, so to her way of thinking, Sarah had no reason to hide her feelings and intentions, other than to play games and gain the upper hand. Devin realized that it was what Sarah had always done.

"Just get to it," Devin finally said, wanting no nonsense.

Sarah looked back at her, surprised by Devin's attitude. She'd honestly thought that Devin had been pining for her in the two years she'd been gone. She decided to try another tactic.

"Well, I was going to ask you for another chance, but…" she let her voice trail off as she held her hands out plaintively.

Devin actually laughed. "Seriously?"

"What's that mean?" Sarah asked, honestly shocked.

"I'm not interested in another chance."

Sarah narrowed her eyes. "You said you loved me."

"I did love you, but when you chose the closet over me, I kinda got over it."

"But things are different now," Sarah said, sounding strangely triumphant.

Devin didn't respond, instead she chewed on the gum she had in her mouth. She knew it would irritate Sarah that she didn't ask, two could play this game.

"I'm different," Sarah said, when she realized Devin wasn't going to ask. "I'm out now."

"Great, I'm happy for you."

"It's what you wanted," Sarah said, cajoling.

"It's what I want for anyone who is hiding who they really are inside."

"It's that pilot, isn't it?" Sarah asked, switching tactics again.

Devin smiled, knowing Sarah was getting desperate now.

"How long have you been dating her?" Sarah asked, clearly jealous.

Devin thought about not answering, since it was really none of Sarah's business, but finally she shrugged. "A few months."

"Months?" Sarah repeated glowering at her. "We were together for years, Devin!"

"Time served doesn't really count after the fact, Sarah."

"You can't even be in love with her. What is she, some washed up Army pilot?"

Devin narrowed her eyes. "You better be careful right now, Sarah. You don't know anything about Skyler, so you'd be smart to keep your mouth shut when it comes to her."

Sarah looked shocked again, this wasn't the easy going party girl she knew from before. Regardless, she decided to push her luck.

"I've never seen a grunt worth much."

"Yeah," Devin said, standing up, "we're done." She left.

Devin told Skyler about her encounter with Sarah later that night as they ate dinner.

Skyler grinned. "Marines aren't too fond of the Army."

"Well, since she's been sitting in Germany, while others like you have been in the war, she needs to shut her fucking mouth," Devin snapped.

Skyler grinned again. "Easy now."

"I don't know why I never saw her for what she is," Devin said, shaking her head.

"What do you mean?"

"She's so manipulative, she plays games to get what she wants, and what she always wants is the upper hand."

Skyler rubbed the bridge of her nose. "I think that's what they teach them in Marine basic."

"Yeah that and, 'When there's gun fire, Marines run toward the bullets! Oorah!'" Devin said, in a pretty good imitation of a Marine.

Skyler chuckled. "Yeah, in the Army they teach us to shoot back."

Devin got a laugh out of that. "I'll have to remember that one for when she calls again."

"She called you after that meeting?" Skyler asked, shocked.

"Five times," Devin replied, holding up her phone.

"I guess they don't teach Marines to take 'no' for an answer, either."

"Guess not."

"Did you answer?"

"No, but I texted her and told her to stop calling me," Devin said.

"Has she called since then?" Skyler asked.

"Nope."

"Maybe she got the hint then."

"Maybe."

Sarah hadn't gotten the hint. Apparently she'd gotten the idea that she just needed to try harder. She continued to call Devin, until Devin blocked her number. Then she started emailing Devin, saying things like, "I just want to apologize for what I said…" which turned to, "So you're just not going to talk to me?" and later, "You will talk to me, Devin!"

It was still going on two days later while Devin was at work. She felt like it was getting ridiculous, and she was beginning to wonder if Sarah was becoming a little unhinged. This concern stepped up a little while later when she got a text from a number she didn't recognize saying, "I'm out front, come talk to me- Sarah."

Devin called Skyler.

"Hey, babe, what's up?" Skyler answered, she was in her car.

"Where are you?"

"I'm in the car, headed south on 405. Why?"

Devin blew her breath out. "Sarah's been calling, texting and emailing me all day," she said, loathe to drag Skyler into this situation, but not sure what else to do.

The last thing she wanted was to involve the LAPD. If Sarah was just trying to be tenacious thinking it would impress Devin, she didn't want to chance the police involvement that would possibly spell an end to her career as a Marine. But at the same time, her turning up outside the police department where she was working, just wasn't cool.

"Okay..." Skyler said her tone leading.

"I blocked her number, so she started emailing me, I ignored the emails and now she's shown up here."

"Seriously?" Skyler asked, starting to signal to move out of the fast lane to head toward the exit, knowing it would be faster to get to Devin that way. "I'm on my way."

"I'm sorry, Sky," Devin said, grimacing on her end, "you seem to have to rescue me constantly these days."

Skyler grinned as she changed freeways. "It's the job"

"Great!" Devin said, rolling her eyes.

"I'll be there as soon as I can. Do not go outside."

Skyler pulled up in front of the building thirty minutes later. She texted Devin to let her know she was there. Then she got out of her car, moved to the passenger side and leaned against the front fender lighting a cigarette, her eyes on the building. Devin had seen her drive up and walked out to meet her. Sarah intercepted her halfway.

"Devin, I just need you to listen to me," Sarah said, holding up her hands.

"I don't need to listen to you, Sarah, you need to leave me alone now," Devin said, shaking inside but keeping her voice strong.

Devin strode toward Skyler.

"Devin, just wait!" Sarah yelled, trying to catch up. She reached out to grab Devin's arm, but stopped short when she saw Skyler.

Skyler looked completely relaxed, her legs stretched out in front of her, crossed at the ankles. She wore faded jeans, her usual combat style boots, and black tank top with a black leather bomber style jacket. She smoked as she watched Sarah approach, trailing Devin. Her eyes trained on the other woman, narrowing slightly in the cigarette smoke she blew out, her head canting slightly, as if trying to figure out what Sarah was doing. Devin went straight to Skyler, leaning in to kiss her soundly on the lips, as Sarah stood by glowering. After the kiss, Devin moved to lean on the car next to Skyler. Skyler's free arm came up to encircle her shoulders.

"Did you need something?" Skyler asked after a few moments.

Sarah gave her a scowl. "I need to talk to Devin."

Skyler nodded, taking another drag on her cigarette, looking like she was considering the request.

"I think she's made it pretty clear she doesn't want to talk to you," Skyler said, glancing down at Devin, who nodded her head in confirmation. "So why don't you just run along back to Pendleton or wherever you're at these days."

"Or what?" Sarah challenged, puffing up her chest in a display of offense.

Skyler didn't answer right away, letting a slow grin spread across her face. "Let's not find out, huh?"

"Oh, big bad Army pilot, what are you gonna do?" Sarah sneered.

Sarah and Skyler were of even height, Sarah had about twenty pounds over Skyler and that made her think she was superior, besides the fact that she was a Marine after all.

Skyler grinned, her look indicating her opinion of Sarah's bluster, like it was absolutely ridiculous.

"I got out of the Army about two and half years ago, and this has nothing to do with the fact that I'm a pilot," Skyler said, amused.

"You think you can take me, grunt?" Sarah practically spat.

Skyler took another drag from her cigarette, her eyes on Sarah. "I think we don't need to find out."

"Afraid I'll kick your ass?" Sarah countered.

Skyler gave a snort of laughter. "No, I just don't want jarhead blood on my car."

Sarah looked like she really wanted to challenge Skyler, but Devin intervened.

"Leave Sarah," Devin said, taking a step forward.

Devin didn't notice that Skyler immediately tossed aside her cigarette, straightening from the car and took a step toward her. She did, however, suddenly feel Skyler standing behind her, and took strength from it. Glancing up and back, she saw that Skyler's eyes were on Sarah, she also noticed the tension in Skyler, even though her face showed nothing of that tension.

"Just go," Devin said then, "or I'll march right back in there and bring out some of my LAPD friends to deal with your ass."

"Brass don't really like police actions. Could cost you your commission." Skyler seconded.

Sarah looked hesitant suddenly. It was apparent she hadn't considered that angle.

"Stalker laws are pretty strong here in LA," Devin said.

"Could cost you your freedom too," Skyler added.

Sarah stepped back then, realizing she was definitely in a bad situation. The Corps was all she knew, losing her commission would get her kicked out. No woman was worth that. With that she pivoted on her heel and walked away.

Devin relaxed instantly. Turning she looked up at Skyler. "You were ready to fight her, weren't you?" she asked, as she slid her arms up around Skyler's neck.

"If she did anything stupid," Skyler said, nodding, as she pulled Devin close.

"Like?"

"Like try to put her hands on you again." Skyler had seen Sarah try to make a grab for Devin.

"That simple?"

"That simple," Skyler confirmed.

Devin stared up at Skyler, thinking that this woman would never cease to surprise her. Most people Devin knew would never have even tried to stand up to someone like Sarah. Skyler wasn't like anyone she knew, she loved that about her.

In the end they left Devin's rental car at the garage, deciding that Skyler would just drive her in the next day.

On the drive back to Devin's house, Devin looked over at Skyler, watching her sing the song that was on in the car; it was "Somewhere I Belong" by Linkin Park. The lyrics talked about being hollow and alone and it being his own fault, repeating the same words over. The chorus talked about wanting to heal and to feel and wanting to find a place to belong.

It was a very somber song, but Devin could see that Skyler felt every word.

Skyler seemed very connected to a lot of the songs that she listened to in the car and at home, so Devin had quickly learned to tune into the songs that Skyler had either turned up, or the ones she sang the words to vehemently.

When the song ended, Skyler predictably reached over to turn the stereo down again. Devin twitched her lips in amusement, wondering if Skyler even realized she did that regularly.

Skyler caught the look on Devin's face. "What?"

Devin smiled, shaking her head. "Nothing," she said, not wanting to let Skyler know that she was on to some of her 'tells.'

Skyler glanced over at her and narrowed her eyes suspiciously, but didn't pursue the subject.

"So do you usually get into fights over girls?" Devin asked a little while later.

Skyler grinned, dropping her head for a second, then looked over at Devin. "Not usually, no."

Devin nodded, with a barely suppressed grin on her lips. "So, this was unusual for you," she asked.

Skyler opened her mouth, then closed it giving her a scathing look.

"You're enjoying this," Skyler said, her tone accusing.

Devin laughed outright, nodding her head. "Is that wrong? That I like the possessive streak?"

Skyler curled her lips in mock disgust. "Yes, it's wrong."

Devin laughed again, nodding.

Skyler just shook her head, even as a smile began.

Chapter 5

As fall turned to winter, the rains increased, causing Skyler to be extremely busy. She grabbed every off moment with Devin she could, but by November she was beyond exhausted. Devin was more concerned about Skyler getting enough sleep than being with her all the time. There had been a few close calls for the team during some rescues and it had been enough to have Devin telling Skyler to just stay at the hangar or her apartment. Devin would come to the apartment when she knew Skyler had slept and had time to spend with her.

Devin often reflected on their relationship; the parts that had evolved and the parts that hadn't. Skyler still had a tendency to keep things in when it came to her past, especially her time in Iraq. From what Devin had gathered from conversations with Jams when Skyler wasn't around, Skyler's personality had changed drastically after Iraq. Devin was now able to sense the looming cloud of depression that lingered around Skyler all the time. There were times when Devin was sure it was creeping closer; she could see it when Skyler would sit outside and smoke. Often Skyler would stare into the distance, her look subdued. There had been many times when Devin had wanted to ask her what she'd been thinking about, but she always hesitated. She'd come to fear the ice cold facade that Skyler could so easily slip into whenever she felt threatened or challenged.

Part of Devin knew that there was a confrontation coming some-day down the road. She knew that at some point she would have to either get Skyler to talk to her about what had happened in Iraq, or she'd have to leave Skyler, or Skyler would leave her. It sat in the darkest part of her heart, and Devin did everything she could to ignore it on a daily basis. She desperately wanted to help Skyler through whatever trauma she'd sustained, but Devin wasn't altogether sure Skyler would let her in that far, even if she did say she loved her.

All Devin wanted to do was cling to the good times with Skyler, and to make more of them. For that reason, by early December, Devin was planning a surprise for Skyler for her birthday which fell on Christmas Eve. She'd talked to Jams and he was helping her plan.

Christmas Eve morning dawned. Skyler and the crew had the night before off, and unbeknownst to Skyler, Jams had arranged that with their Commanding Officer. So Devin showed up early Christmas Eve morning to wake Skyler.

Walking into Skyler's bedroom, Devin stood watching her girl-friend sleep. In the six months they'd been dating, Devin was amazed by the fact that she still found Skyler incredibly sexy; it was rare since Devin tended to get bored with women easily. So the fact that Skyler could hold her interest told Devin that this was something special.

Watching Skyler now, Devin noted that Skyler seemed to always sleep with one arm above her head, except when they slept together. For a woman that had purposely distanced herself from Devin six months before, after they'd slept together that first time, Skyler certainly stayed in close contact with Devin now when they slept. Devin took that as a good sign for their relationship.

As usual, when Devin stood staring at her for too long, Skyler sensed it and woke up.

"Well, hello there," Skyler said.

Devin walked over to the bed, setting her purse down by the bed, and leaning down to kiss Skyler's lips. Skyler reached up, pulling Devin down to kiss her more deeply. Before long the fire ignited between them and it was another hour before Devin remembered why she was there.

"Happy birthday, by the way," Devin said, reaching up to touch Skyler's cheek.

They lay naked in bed, their bodies still partially intertwined.

"How did you know it was my birthday?"

Devin gave her a look that said, *Really?*

"That son of a bitch!" Skyler said, even as she grinned.

Devin chuckled, even as she moved to reach down to her purse and pull out an envelope. She handed the large manila envelope to Skyler.

"What's this?" Skyler asked.

"An envelope."

"Smart ass."

"Open it!"

Skyler opened the envelope and was surprised by all the things in it. When she simply poked at the items, not taking them out of the envelope, Devin got impatient.

"Oh, God, let me do that!" she said, sitting up and pulling the sheet up with her.

Skyler chuckled, as she moved to sit up as well.

Devin took one thing at a time out of the envelope. The first was a birthday card, which Skyler read, smiling softly at the sweet sentiment of the card. Then Devin took a folded piece of paper out and handed it to her. Skyler unfolded the paper, and read what it said. It was the confirmation for two first class tickets on a flight to Las Vegas, leaving in three hours.

"Vegas?" Skyler asked, raising her eyebrow at Devin.

"Yeah," Devin said, smiling, "you need some fun."

Skyler looked back at her, pressing her lips together, looking apologetic. "Babe, this is really sweet, but…"

"Jams already arranged for time off for you with your CO."

Skyler looked back her, happily surprised. "Wow, okay."

"Okay, next," Devin said, reaching into the envelope again.

"There's more?" Skyler asked, sounding flabbergasted.

"It's your birthday!"

The next folded piece of paper had hotel confirmation information.

Skyler gave Devin a sidelong look. "What is 'The Mansion at MGM Grand'?"

"It's a hotel room."

Skyler looked at the paper narrowing her eyes at a particular part of it. "Why is this part blacked out?"

Devin licked her lips, smiling at the same time, her eyes twinkling mischievously. "It's rude to leave price tags on gifts, Skyler Boché."

"Hmmm…" Skyler murmured, her suspicions high at that point. "Is that five days?"

"Yes, five days. You need a vacation Skyler. I would have happily taken you anywhere, but I know it'll take longer and I want you to have time to relax."

Skyler looked back at her, very touched that she'd considered that fact. Leaning forward she kissed Devin's lips, her hand reaching up to caress her cheek.

Pulling back slightly, she looked into Devin's eyes. "Thank you honey."

Skyler was floored by the gift, it was so extravagant.

That stunned feeling only grew a few hours later as they boarded a plane and sat in first class. It grew exponentially when a limo met them at the airport and drove them to their hotel. When the limo stopped, and the driver opened the door for them, Skyler stepped out and found herself completely speechless.

They stood in front of not a hotel, but an incredible vision of elegance. The Tuscany villa-inspired architecture was incredible. There was a courtyard filled with trees and beautiful flowers, at the center of which was a huge fountain. The building's stonework was elegant, with terraces and eighteenth century style lighting. Skyler had never seen such a beautiful place that was considered a hotel.

"Devin…" Skyler breathed as she wound her arms around Devin's waist, hugging her from behind, staring at the villa entrance.

"You like it?" Devin asked smiling as she glanced back at Skyler.

"It's amazing," Skyler said, sounding every bit as awed as she felt.

Devin giggled. "Good, 'cause you're really going to like the inside!"

Skyler allowed herself to be led into through the entrance of the hotel, looking a bit bewildered. An hour later she was sure she couldn't handle any more surprises. The room they were in was larger than her apartment and a hundred times more elegant.

Laying back on the huge bed, strewn with rose petals, Skyler looked up at Devin, who stood looking down at her with a smile.

"Now I know why that price tag was blacked out," Skyler said, her tone sly.

Devin didn't reply, only grinning in response.

The room was so elegantly appointed, Skyler had no idea what to do with herself. She walked around examining everything from the artwork to the statues, touching the dining room table reverently, and just shaking her head at the size of the bathroom with its marble enclosed shower and huge bathing tub. The room also featured its own sauna and steam room. Additionally it had its own pantry and a private entrance. Skyler was blown away. She'd never even imagined this kind of opulence, let alone staying in it for five days.

She was further bowled over when they left the hotel a little while later to go check out the sites, and waiting there was a brand new Nissan GTR, a car that Skyler had long envied. A man stood by the car and handed Devin a clipboard as she walked up, she signed a paper, and he handed Devin the keys.

Devin turned and handed the keys to Skyler. "Ours to drive for the trip."

"Oh, my God…" Skyler said, as her hands touched the fender of the car with so much reverence that it was almost painful to watch.

Skyler looked at Devin then. "We get to drive this? The whole time?"

"*You* get to drive this, the whole time," Devin said, emphasizing the word "you."

Skyler swept Devin up in her arms, kissing her and twirling them around. Devin laughed, loving that she'd made Skyler this happy.

When they got into the car, Skyler just sat with her hands on the steering wheel, looking at everything, like a little kid at Christmas.

"My, God, babe, this trip must have cost you a fortune…" Skyler finally said, looking over at Devin.

"Your reaction is worth every penny."

Skyler bit her lip as she reached down to push the start button for the car. Devin was sure Skyler was going to die in ecstasy when the car started with a deep rumble.

"Oh, honey, honey…" Skyler whispered, and Devin was fairly certain, by the rapt look on Skyler's face, that she wasn't talking to her.

Skyler spent the evening thoroughly enjoying the drive. She even got out onto the open road to 'open her up' at one point. Devin spent the evening thoroughly enjoying watching Skyler have the time of her life.

After Skyler had spent two hours putting the GTR through its paces, Devin asked if she was ready for dinner.

"I could eat."

"Okay," Devin said, reaching out to engage the navigation system in the GTR, putting in an address and giving it the command to go.

Skyler looked at her expectantly.

"What?" Devin asked.

"Where are we going?" Skyler asked.

"Just go where she tells you."

Skyler rolled her eyes, unable to believe the lengths Devin had gone to in order to plan this trip for her. It downright amazed her.

When they arrived at their destination Skyler was confused. They were back at the hotel.

"Room service?" Skyler queried, sounding hopeful.

"Nope," Devin said, as the valet opened her door for her.

Skyler got out on her side, tossing the keys to the valet with a wink. "Be nice to her," she said, running her hand over the hood as she walked around the car.

The valet laughed, nodding his head.

Devin took Skyler by the hand and headed into the hotel. They walked through the hotel and up the escalator. When Devin came to a stop, Skyler saw the restaurant. They were in front of Emeril's New Orleans Fish House, it was known for its Cajun cuisine.

Skyler looked over at Devin. "Do you even like Cajun food?"

"Never tried it," Devin replied with a shrug, "but Jams said you love it, so I thought it was a good place for your birthday dinner."

Skyler shook her head, so completely baffled by Devin.

"What?" Devin asked, looking up at Skyler.

Skyler turned to Devin, putting her arms around the girl and pulling her in close to kiss her deeply.

"You think of everything, don't you?" she asked when their lips parted.

"I try," Devin said, basking in Skyler's attention.

"You succeed," Skyler said unequivocally.

Taking Devin's hand, Skyler walked up to the counter where the hostess stood.

"Hi," the hostess said, smiling at both of them.

"We have a reservation," Devin said, "under Boché."

Skyler pursed her lips for a moment, grinning, for some reason she liked that Devin had put it under her last name.

"Right this way," the hostess said, taking them into the restaurant.

They skirted the circular bar in the middle of the restaurant and headed toward the more private dining area. The restaurant was alive with colors: reds, teals, and vivid purples. The décor was kitschy, but definitely with a New Orleans flavor to it, Skyler liked it immediately. They were seated in a booth and handed the menus.

Skyler looked at the menu and was sure she'd died and gone to Heaven. The menu included all the classics, like gumbo, shrimp bowl and crawfish, but it also included some of Emeril's signature dishes, many of which sounded good too.

Devin watched Skyler's face as she read the menu, seeing that she was going to have a hard time choosing. When she looked at the menu, she had no idea what to try. She'd never thought of trying something like crawfish and was pretty sure she wouldn't like it, but this wasn't her night, it was Skyler's.

Within minutes the manager of the restaurant came up to the table. He smiled at them, extending his hand to each of them.

"I'm Sean," he said, his green eyes twinkling, "I'm the general manager. I understand you're celebrating a birthday tonight."

Devin nodded, pointing at Skyler.

"On behalf of Emeril's, let me wish you bonne anniversaire," he said with a flourish and a slight bow.

"Merci," Skyler said, inclining her head, saying "Thank you."

"Très bien," the manager replied, smiling widely.

"You speak French," Skyler said, nodding.

"Some," he replied, nodding.

"Your accent is good," Skyler said.

"Merci beaucoup," he replied. "I take it you're from Louisiana?" Pronouncing it *Lousina* as the locals do.

"Baton Rouge," Skyler replied, saying it the Cajun way, winking at Devin as she saw her make a face.

"Aw, oui," he said, smiling and nodding. "Please enjoy yourselves," he said then. "And if there is anything I can do for you ladies, please don't hesitate to let me know."

"We will," Devin said, smiling warmly, "thank you."

As the manager walked away, Devin looked over at Skyler. "Well, that was fun," she said smiling.

"What was?"

"Getting to hear your accent again,"

"Oh lord," Skyler said, rolling her eyes.

"So what are you going to order?" Devin asked, biting her lip in indecision.

Skyler looked over at her for a long moment, her look speculative. "Gonna let me pay for dinner?"

"Nope," Devin replied immediately.

Skyler wrinkled her nose and pursed her lips in distaste, looking like she wanted to argue, but then shrugged and looked at her menu again.

Devin narrowed her eyes at her girlfriend. "Don't even think about going chintzy on what you order Skyler."

Skyler looked over at her, her eyes wide with contrived innocence. "I don't know what you mean."

"Yes you do, you little brat," Devin said, scolding.

Skyler grinned unrepentantly.

"Look," Devin said, putting her hand on the table between them, "just so you can stop worrying about the money. I made two hundred thousand on my last job and it was a two-week job. You don't even want to know how much the LAPD is paying me, okay?"

Skyler looked back at Devin for a full minute, her mouth hanging open slightly at the number Devin had thrown out. Finally, she closed her mouth and shook her head.

"I'm in the wrong fuckin' business."

"No," Devin said, putting her hand on Skyler's arm, "you're in the right business, you save lives, that matters more than anything else."

"Doesn't pay for room service though," Skyler countered.

"That's what you have me for," Devin replied with a wink.

Putting down her menu, Skyler turned to face Devin, taking her hands and looking her in the eye. "That is not what I have you for. You do know that, right?"

"Yes, Sky, I do," Devin said, squeezing Skyler's hands in hers.

Skyler looked back at her, her eyes searching Devin's for any sign of misunderstanding. "You just need to know that."

"I do," Devin said, leaning in to kiss Skyler softly, "I do, okay?"

Skyler nodded, drawing in a deep breath and expelling it slowly.

"Why does this bother you so much?" Devin asked, glancing up as the waitress passed.

Skyler looked pensive for a moment. "I guess I'm not used to someone else paying for things."

Devin nodded, having suspected that was the case. "You usually make more than the women you date?"

Skyler chuckled. "Never really mattered."

"Even if they made more, you paid?"

Skyler reached up rubbed her thumb at her lower lip. Devin caught the sign for 'too many questions' and eased away from the subject.

"Anyway, order whatever you want, and if I think you're being sneaky, I'll order everything on the menu."

"Yes ma'am,"

Devin chuckled at the response.

It was a good night.

On their second day in Vegas, Devin insisted that they do some gambling. She found that Skyler was actually pretty good at poker, and within a couple of hours they were up by over a thousand dollars.

"Guess it pays to have that cool facade, huh?" Devin asked.

"Made me a lot of money in the Army," Skyler replied with a wink.

"Oh my!" Devin replied, widening her eyes.

They had just had lunch and made their way back to their room.

"So what do you want to do tonight?" Devin asked.

Skyler caught the look and gave her a suspicious look back. "Why do I think you already know what you want us to do?"

"Well, I have an idea," Devin said, walking over to the dining room table to set her purse down, being overly casual. Skyler picked up on it instantly.

Walking over, she stood behind Devin, her arms circling her waist and pulling her back against her. She nuzzled the side of Devin's head, kissing her temple, then her ear.

"We can do whatever you want," Skyler whispered.

Devin turned in Skyler's arms, winding her arms up around Skyler's neck. "Would you want to go to a club?"

Skyler looked back at her for a long moment, but then nodded. "If that's what you want to do, then yes, let's do it."

"Yay!" Devin said, smiling.

Later that evening they'd agreed to get dressed separately, Devin said she wanted to surprise Skyler. It was definitely effective. Skyler stood staring at her girlfriend in shock. Devin wore a black halter dress that exposed a great deal of skin, and definitely a lot of leg. It hugged her perfectly, in all the right places. On her feet she wore black strappy heels.

"Wow," Skyler said, looking duly impressed. "You look amazing."

"So do you," Devin replied.

Devin was definitely shocked by Skyler's outfit, it was unlike anything she'd ever seen her in before. She wore black jeans with black heeled, but still combat style, boots. She also wore a light teal colored shirt that was close fitted and just about the same color as her eyes, with a fitted but long black blazer over it with the sleeves pushed up. She also wore a black, thick banded watch on her wrist and around her neck she wore a silver chain with a set of black dog tags, one of which had silver angel wings engraved in it.

Walking over to Skyler, Devin reached up touching the dog tags, she saw that the second tag had the initials "T.O." and "B.K." engraved in silver script. She smiled as she touched the tags, then looked up at Skyler who was watching her.

"You look so…" she began, "wow," she added when she couldn't come up with another word.

Skyler smiled, leaning down to kiss her lips. "I'm gonna have to watch you every second."

Devin smiled at that. "Good, you won't be able to look at anyone else that way."

"As if I would."

Devin looked at her for a long moment, canting her head slightly. "That's really not your way, is it?" she asked, even though her tone indicated it really wasn't a question.

Skyler shook her head, confirming, "No."

Devin found that she loved that about Skyler. She never had to worry about her girlfriend looking at other women. Now women coming on to Skyler; that was rampant. It was part of the reason she'd chosen a regular club instead of a gay one.

Walking up to the club an hour later, Devin was shocked when the large bouncer at the door yelled, "Voodoo!" when he saw Skyler.

The man was huge, with what Devin would describe as tree trunks for arms; he wasn't fat, he was all muscle and very tall. He had a shock of blond hair and a big smile for Skyler.

"Acorn!" Skyler replied, laughing as they hugged.

"How you be?" Acorn asked.

"I'm alright. This where you landed?"

"My ex is here with my kid, so yeah," Acorn replied, shrugging.

"Sorry to hear that, man," Skyler said, remembering that his wife had been a real pain in the ass while they'd been overseas, but he'd loved her all the same.

"And who's this?" Acorn said, his big blue eyes going to Devin.

"This is my girlfriend, Devin," she said, gesturing to the man. "This is Acorn."

"Acorn?" Devin repeated expectantly.

"His last name is Oak," Skyler said, grinning. "Crews aren't too creative sometimes."

"Nope!" Acorn boomed, nodding to people as they got impatient with the reunion.

He took a couple more IDs looking at Skyler, his look searching. Devin suspected that whoever this man was, he knew something about

Skyler's time in Iraq. She could tell he was trying to decide what to ask about and what not to.

"So," Acorn said as the door slowed down again, "where'd you land? And what happened to that hot little number?"

Skyler looked back at him for a long moment, then rolled her eyes, shaking her head, the man had absolutely no edit function, he never had.

"Did I introduce my girlfriend?"

"Yeah, Voodoo, yeah, but what—"

"We're not together anymore," Skyler put in, smiling despite her sharp tone.

"Cool, cool," Acorn said, putting his hands out to mollify Skyler's tone. "So where ya workin'?"

"LAFD," Skyler replied.

"Air ops of course," Acorn put in.

"Roger that."

"Jams with ya there?" Acorn asked.

"Can't get rid of him."

"Doh!" Acorn said, laughing. "Well get on in," he said, waving them into the club, "no cover for vets."

"Thanks man," Skyler said, holding her hand out to him.

He took it shaking it, and winking at Devin.

Inside the club, they found a table, and Skyler went to the bar to get them drinks. When she returned there were two men standing at the table talking to Devin. Skyler drew in a deep breath, expelling it in exasperation; she'd known Devin was bound to cause trouble wherever she went in that dress.

"Boys," Skyler said, as she walked up, her eyes looking from one to the other.

She moved to stand next to where Devin sat on the high bar chair. Skyler leaned in to kiss her lips, then looked back at the men standing there, a mild challenge in her eyes. They looked like sailors, with their short crew cuts and the "squidly swagger" as Skyler saw it. Both men did a little bit of shuffling, but neither of them walked away.

Oh lordy, here we go… Skyler thought to herself, even as she glanced down at Devin.

She looked back at the men then. "Did you need something?" she asked, her tone an easy drawl, much as it had been with Sarah a few months earlier.

Devin recognized that it was designed to not only challenge, but also to warn whoever she was dealing with. She grimaced as one of the men detected the challenge and apparently wasn't the back down type.

"We were just talking to the lady," the shorter of the two men said, his tone bordering on accusing.

Skyler nodded, lifting her beer and taking a drink, her look considering. "You're done talking to her."

"Who says?" replied the taller of the two, who was still only as tall as Skyler.

Skyler's look shifted to the man, her look confident, even as she set her beer down on the table.

"Yeah, she seemed pretty into it," the second man put in.

Skyler nodded, a grin curling her lips as she looked down at Devin. "Are you into it now, babe?"

"No, I'm good," Devin said smiling, even as she prayed that her statement would end it.

No such luck.

"Now wait a minute," the shorter guy standing on the other side of Devin began, as he reached out to touch Devin's arm.

"I wouldn't do that," Skyler told the man.

"No?" the guy said, his look taking on a challenge as he reached for Devin.

Skyler took a step back to step around the chair Devin was in, the taller guy grabbed her arm to stop her.

"You need to remove your hand, now," Skyler growled at the guy. Her tone become very low, the look on her face should have warned the man that she was deadly serious, but he didn't see that.

The movement, had, however halted the other guy from grabbing at Devin.

The man holding Skyler's arm asked, "What's a matter, honey?" He moved his hand from her arm to her shoulder. "You don't want to share?"

Devin saw it happen, she saw a switch flip in Skyler's eyes, she had a split second to yell Skyler's name and then it happened.

With a speed that Devin could barely follow, Skyler reached across herself grabbing the hand on her shoulder and then brought her other arm up and through slamming down on the man's elbow. She continued to hold the hand that had been on her shoulder bending it painfully at the wrist as she yanked it in front of her, putting the man

119

off balance. She then proceeded to take him down to the ground, slamming him hard into the floor. She put her knee on his back keeping his arm up behind him.

"Son of a bitch!" said the guy standing next to Devin.

"She warned him," Devin said simply, as the area around them erupted in cheers and applause.

"Get the fuck off!" screamed the guy on the floor, as a pool of blood started to form from his nose.

Acorn was there then, assisting Skyler and taking over, to yank the guy up off the floor.

"You broke my nose you bitch!" the guy yelled. "I want that bitch arrested!"

"The way I saw it," Acorn said, his look considering, "was you who assaulted her, she just defended herself."

"Bullshit!" yelled the guy's friend. "We were just being friendly!"

"Too friendly, it looks like," Acorn said. With that he escorted both men to the door.

People standing nearby eyed Skyler with a mixture of awe and respect. Skyler didn't even seem to notice; she'd gone back to drinking her beer as if nothing had happened. The only way Devin could tell she was affected at all was when Skyler went to light a cigarette, she could see her hands were still shaking a bit.

Reaching out she took Skyler's free hand holding it in both of hers.

Later that night on the drive back to the hotel, Devin found she had to ask questions.

"How the hell did you do that back there?" she asked, still astounded by Skyler's agility. She'd long suspected that Skyler was a lot tougher than she let on; the term 'metal under tension' came to mind.

"You mean putting our little friend down?" Skyler asked, grinning.

"Yeah, that," Devin said, smiling at the phrase "putting our little friend down."

Skyler shrugged. "Experience."

"In the Army?"

"In the Army, in life…"

"You've had to defend yourself like that other times too?" Devin asked, shocked at the idea.

"I told you, I've felt different my whole life, even when I was a kid. Other kids know when someone is different, so I had to learn how to fight early."

"Oh my God, Skyler…"

"It's not a big deal."

"It's not what a normal life is like," Devin said. "That's a really rough childhood."

"You have no idea," Skyler said, sadly and seriously.

Devin looked over at her, sensing there was more to what she was saying, but also sensing that it wasn't the time to ask those questions, so she decided to change topics.

"So, what about that 'hot little number' Acorn was referring to?"

"Oh, Jesus," Skyler said, laughing out loud.

"Well?"

"She's an ex,"

"Okay…" Devin said, her tone leading. When Skyler wasn't forthcoming with any details she said, "Come on, you know all about one of my exes."

"That's because she showed up!"

"Well, what if this one showed up?"

"Uh," Skyler said, rubbing the bridge of her nose, "if that one shows up, I'd suggest you duck."

"What does that mean?" Devin asked, her eyes widening.

"She's rather, um, passionate."

"How passionate?"

"Well, not boil your bunny, passionate, but definitely throwing things at your head when she's pissed, passionate."

"Yikes!" Devin said. "She threw things at you?"

"She cleared an entire coffee table of its contents once, throwing it at me."

"Did she hit you?"

"Fortunately, part of the requirement of being a pilot is fast reaction time, so I ducked pretty well."

"So you guys fought?" Devin asked.

"Oh yeah." Skyler rolled her eyes.

"About what?"

"Everything," Skyler said, but when Devin looked like she was waiting for more, she continued, "she was very jealous, so she was convinced I was cheating on her constantly."

"How long were you two together?"

"All and all about three years."

"Wow!" Devin said, surprised by the length of time.

"You gotta know that part of that time included an eighteen-month deployment to Iraq."

"Oh," Devin said, nodding. "So you guys fought, and she threw things at you."

"Yeah, threw things, caused scenes, got into fights with other girls that she was convinced I was screwing behind her back."

Devin just looked back at her a moment, then shook her head.

"What?" Skyler asked, having seen the look.

"I'm just surprised."

"What do you mean?"

"I just wouldn't think you'd put up with that kind of thing." Devin said.

Skyler grinned, her look considering. "Well, I used to," she said, her tone telling Devin that this was something else that had changed since her time in Iraq.

Devin nodded, not wanting to poke her too much on that subject, but needing to know one thing.

"Did you love her?" she asked, surprised at how much the answer meant to her.

Skyler hesitated for a long moment, then shook her head. "No, I didn't. I mean, things with her were hot and passionate, but no, I didn't love her."

Devin nodded, looking over at Skyler again. She realized she was relieved by what Skyler had said.

"Was she in love with you?" Devin asked.

Skyler didn't answer for a long moment, then she shrugged. "I guess you'd have to ask her that."

Devin looked over at Skyler. "Did she tell you that she was in love with you?"

Skyler glanced at her, her look surprised. "Yeah, she did."

"But you didn't believe her?"

"It's not that..."

"Then?"

"I just think it's easier for some people to be in love than others."

Devin looked over at Skyler. "But that's not you, is it?"

"No," Skyler replied.

Devin let that word go straight to her heart. She was fairly sure that Skyler had no idea how much what she'd just said meant to her. She cherished the thought that even though Skyler didn't love easily, Skyler loved her. It meant so much to her, it scared her that it did.

That night back at the hotel, Devin relished their lovemaking even more. As they lay together afterwards, Devin shocked Skyler by asking, "What's her name?"

"What?" Skyler asked, her mind having been somewhere completely different.

"The ex."

Skyler chuckled. "Seriously?"

"Yeah," Devin said, turning her head to look at Skyler.

"Rose."

"Where does she live?"

"LA," Skyler said, narrowing her eyes at Devin. "Don't hack her."

Devin looked back at Skyler, the picture of innocence, even as a slow grin spread across her lips.

Skyler shook her head, rolling her eyes. *God help Rose,* she thought. She knew that even without a last name, Devin could pull together enough to probably find the girl.

Later that night as they slept, Skyler suddenly jerked awake, sitting upright and breathing heavily. Devin turned over to look at her.

"Sky?" she queried tiredly.

"It's okay," Skyler said, getting her breathing under control, "just a bad dream."

"You sure?" Devin asked, unable to really see Skyler's face in the dim light of the room.

"Yeah, babe, I'm fine," Skyler said, leaning down to kiss her. "I'll be right back."

"Okay."

Skyler got out of bed, pulling on her jeans and a tank top.

Outside the room, on the private patio, she lit a cigarette with shaking hands. She took deep drags trying to calm her nerves. The dream had been vivid and it had scared the hell out of her. After three cigarettes she finally felt calm enough to go back to bed. It took a while to fall asleep again, fortunately Devin didn't wake when she came back into the room, she was grateful for that.

Their last night in Vegas, they decided to try a gay club. The club was called Free Zone, it was low key and mostly frequented by gay men; for the most part, exclusively lesbian clubs were non-existent. The fact that it was a club for men, primarily, was good as far as Devin was concerned, since she figured she'd have a lot less trouble keeping tabs on Skyler, less women hitting on her. She found out not too long after they'd gotten there that she was wrong, but for a completely different reason.

They'd been at the bar for about a half an hour, when Devin saw Skyler freeze, her beer halfway to her lips. Her eyes were focused over Devin's right shoulder, so Devin turned and looked to see if she could see what Skyler was focused on. It took a minute to locate her in the menagerie of half-naked men all over the place, but when she saw the woman, she knew there was something there, because the woman was staring at Skyler as well.

"Son of a…" Skyler muttered as the woman started toward them.

"Who is that?" Devin started to ask, but the woman got over to them in that time.

The woman was without a doubt one of the most beautiful women Devin had ever seen. She was Hispanic, with big dark eyes and a swing of thick silky looking black hair. The outfit she wore left little to the imagination and a lot of dark-toned, smooth skin on display. Boy did she have a body! Devin never worried about her body, she knew hers was pretty decent, but suddenly she felt like a fat slob standing near this woman. *Who is that?* Devin thought in frustration.

"Skyler," the woman said, her accent thick.

Skyler looked back at the woman, lifting the beer to her lips and taking a drink. "Rose."

So that's Rose?! Devin thought. Skyler didn't slouch when it came to women, did she?

Rose's eyes narrowed at Skyler, but then moved to Devin quizzically.

Devin caught the curl of Skyler's lips, but then looked back at the woman who was visibly assessing her.

"Rose, this is Devin," Skyler put in, her tone even.

"I see," Rose said, with a spark of jealousy in her eyes instantly.

"Easy…" Skyler said, her tone low, as her eyes stared right into Rose's.

"You threatening me, Skyler?" Rose said, her tone sharp.

"I'm warning you,"

Rose gave a short laugh, then looked at Devin again. "Good luck holding on to her," she said, snidely.

"Haven't had any trouble so far," Devin countered, her look assured.

Skyler grinned at that, even as she pulled out a cigarette to light it.

"Still smoking, I see," Rose said, seeming to be happy to find another topic to move to.

Skyler took a deep drag, then blew the smoke out toward Rose. Rose instantly narrowed her eyes, her stance changing slightly indicating an imminent attack.

Skyler canted her head to the side, noting the stance. "Haven't changed I see."

"Neither have you!" Rose practically spat.

127

Skyler didn't respond, merely rocking back on her heels, her eyes on Rose's. After a long moment, Rose relaxed her stance.

"You deal with your shit yet?" Rose asked, her look changing to malicious.

Skyler's chin came up instantly, indicating to Devin that this was a sore subject. Devin looked at Skyler, and she could see the ice cold mask fall over her face. She didn't answer Rose's question.

Rose gave a short laugh, her pretty face contorted in a nasty line. It was obvious she wanted to hurt Skyler in any way she could. "That's what I figured,"

With that, Rose gave Devin a dismissive look, then turned and walked away from them. Devin watched her go. Rose joined her friends out on the dance floor, launching into a very sexy style of dance, her look directed at Skyler the whole time.

When Devin turned to look at Skyler, she could see that Skyler was still affected by what Rose had said. When she lifted the cigarette to her mouth again, Devin could see that her hand was shaking ever so slightly.

"Was she actually referring to the crash?" Devin asked, her tone disbelieving.

Skyler grimaced slightly and nodded, taking another deep drag from her cigarette.

"Jesus…" Devin breathed, thinking that the woman had a lot of nerve.

Rose had used the term "shit" like the crash wasn't that big of a deal. Devin wondered how much Rose really knew about it. The idea that she thought it was something that Skyler should just get over, was insane to Devin. How could Rose not know that Skyler had been very damaged by whatever had happened. It was one thing to not know that much about it, and refer to it that way, but Rose didn't seem to understand it at all.

"Do you want to leave?" Devin asked Skyler after a few minutes.

Skyler shook her head. "I'm okay."

"What were the odds of her being here?" Devin asked, wondering at that.

Skyler shrugged, grinning. "She's like the Devil, you say her name and it conjures her up."

Devin laughed at that. "Did you two come here before?"

"Yeah," Skyler said, "once, for our birthdays."

"Birthdays?"

"She was born in the same month as me."

"Oh…"

An hour later, Devin went to the restroom. When she came out of the stall she wasn't very surprised to see Rose standing at the sinks.

Devin walked over to the sink, washed her hands and then dried them.

"So, you think you can hold on to her, huh?" Rose said, her arms crossed over her chest.

Devin turned to lean on the sink, facing Rose. "What makes you think I can't?"

"That chica has too much going on in her head," Rose said, tapping her finger to her own head.

"She's been through a traumatic event," Devin countered, her tone baffled.

"Yeah, yeah, I know," Rose said, waving Devin's comment aside airily.

"I honestly don't think you do."

"You think you know her better than me?" Rose asked, her tone sharpening.

"In this case, yeah, I do."

Rose narrowed her eyes at Devin, her lips flattened into a hard line.

"She'll leave you, just like she did me, you wait and see." Rose practically shrieked, then turned and huffed out of the bathroom.

Devin watched her go, taken aback by the vehemence and conviction the woman had spoken with, part of her wondered if she was right. When Devin left the bathroom she found Skyler just outside waiting for her.

"Everything okay?" Skyler asked, having seen Rose storm out of the bathroom moments earlier.

"Sure," Devin said, grinning, "were you coming to my rescue?"

"Only if I needed to."

"I think I'm done with the club now."

"Let's go."

Their last night in Vegas was spent in the hotel bar, having drinks and eating appetizers. There was no drama, no exes, and no men hitting on them. When they made it to their room they made love until the early hours of the morning and the next day left Vegas behind.

Chapter 6

The months that followed the trip to Vegas were busy for both Devin and Skyler, but they saw each other as often as they could. There were moments when Skyler would pull away from Devin, and Devin made a point of letting her when she needed to be alone. Often she would try to talk to Skyler about whatever had happened that had caused the distance between them, but to no avail and it usually ended in a fight. Devin didn't want to be pushy about Skyler's past, but eventually, something had to give. She couldn't run away from it forever. It wasn't healthy for their relationship to keep dodging problems. Most of the time, the fight would end with Devin backing off and Skyler eventually coming around and apologize.

Three months after they'd gone to Vegas, Devin got a surprising phone call when she was at work. Looking at the display she was surprised to see that the person calling was Amy, someone who was in the Marines with Sarah.

Picking up the call she said, "Hello?"

"Hi Devin," Amy said, her voice sounding serious.

"Hi, Amy," Devin said. "How are you?"

"I'm okay," Amy said, "but I wanted to call you about Sarah."

"Okay…" Devin said, letting her voice trail off to indicate her caution.

"I'm sorry," Amy said, sounding like she really was, "but I thought you should know about this."

"Okay," Devin repeated.

Amy said, "I know you two are kind of on the outs, but I thought you should know that she tried to kill herself last night."

"Holy shit," Devin said, surprised in spite of herself.

"Yeah, that's what I said."

"What did she do?" Devin asked still in shock.

Sarah had always been very self-assured, even if she hadn't been willing to be herself when it came to being gay. Devin had always attributed that to the fact that Sarah's father was a hard core Marine and that there was little chance of him accepting that his daughter was gay. For Sarah to feel so low as to give in to the idea of taking her own life, it wasn't something that Devin would have believed possible.

"She took a half a bottle of painkillers," Amy said. "She claims that she wasn't trying to kill herself, but who takes like twenty Norco accidentally?"

"No one."

"And I hate to tell you this, but I really think it had everything to do with you."

"Me? Why? I haven't even seen her in months."

"That's the thing," Amy said, "I really think she had it in her head that the only thing keeping you two apart was the fact that she wasn't out. So when she came out, she figured she'd get you back."

"Well, I moved on," Devin said, her tone defensive.

"I know. I just don't think she could handle it."

Devin took a deep breath, blowing it out in dismay.

"So why are you telling me this?" Devin asked, sounding resigned.

Amy shrugged on her end, "I guess I thought you should know."

"Because she tried to kill herself over me?"

"Because she's lying to herself and everyone else about it, and I'm worried about her," Amy countered.

Devin nodded, taking that statement in. Amy was Sarah's best friend, and if she was worried about Sarah, she probably had good reason to be worried. It put Devin in a difficult spot though and she wasn't sure there was a lot she could do for Sarah.

"I don't know what or if I can do anything at this point," Devin said, her tone softer.

"I understand," Amy said, knowing that Devin's current girlfriend may not want Devin interacting or helping an ex-girlfriend. Emotional connections were always dangerous territory in the ex-girlfriend department; it didn't take much to ruin a current relationship. Women tended to overthink things when it came to emotional connections, and lesbians were no different.

Later that night Skyler and Devin were in Skyler's car, going to dinner when Devin brought up the phone call.

"So I got a call today," Devin said, her tone purposely casual.

Skyler detected the tone right away and glanced over at her.

"And?" Skyler asked, mildly.

Devin took a deep breath, blowing it out slowly. "It was from a mutual friend of mine and Sarah's, her name is Amy."

Skyler nodded, her look unreadable.

"She said that Sarah tried to kill herself last night."

Skyler's face reflected surprise and shock. "Wow."

"Yeah," Devin said, nodding, "that was kind of my reaction too."

"But she's okay?" Skyler asked, actually looking concerned, which surprised Devin.

"Yes and no," Devin said, biting her lower lip in uncertainty.

"What does that mean?" Skyler asked, gently.

"Amy said she's worried about her," Devin said. "It's not good that Amy is saying that. They're best friends and if Sarah is scaring Amy, it's definitely serious."

Skyler looked over at her, her brows furrowed. "Babe, anyone who tries to kill themselves should always be taken seriously."

"I know, but..." Devin said, shrugging as she let her voice trail off, "not everyone thinks like that."

"Like what?"

"That people who try to kill themselves should be taken seriously. Some people think of people like that as cowards, or like they are just begging for attention."

"People who threaten to kill themselves are issuing a cry for help," Skyler said, her tone serious. "But people who go right ahead and try it without even asking for help are serious about doing it. And that should always be taken seriously."

Devin looked over at Skyler, somehow surprised that she felt so strongly about the subject, but also very glad that Skyler wasn't the type of person who judged people like Sarah, who'd tried suicide. It made her love Skyler more.

"So what are you going to do?" Skyler asked after a few minutes of silence.

"What do you mean?" Devin asked, surprised by the question.

"Well, I assume we're talking about this because you want to help her."

Devin bit her lip, wondering if this was going to become an issue now. Skyler glanced over at Devin when she didn't answer, and caught the look of concern in her eyes.

"I'm saying you should," Skyler said.

"You really think so?"

"Do you want to?"

Devin had to think about that question. Finally she nodded. "Yeah, I think I do."

Skyler nodded. "Then you should."

"And you're okay with that?"

Skyler looked over at her again, her eyes searching Devin's. "I'm okay with you helping her, everyone deserves help."

Devin looked perplexed at that answer, but she nodded.

They arrived at the restaurant a little while later, so they moved on to other topics. Devin kept looking for any sign that Skyler was irritated by the idea of her making contact with Sarah again, but she could detect nothing.

The next day, Devin called Sarah.

Sarah picked up after five rings, her tone when she answered the phone indicated that she hadn't really wanted to pick up.

"Devin?" Sarah queried cautiously.

"Yes," Devin said, smiling in spite of herself.

There was silence on the other end of the line for at least a minute.

"Amy called you," Sarah stated flatly.

"Yes, she called me," Devin said, softening her voice.

On the other end of the line, Sarah closed her eyes in shame.

"She shouldn't have done that," Sarah said, her voice affected.

Devin was sure she could hear tears in Sarah's voice.

"Yes, she should have," Devin said.

"I'm fine," Sarah said, her voice flat.

"Uh-huh," Devin said, unconvinced.

"I am."

"Okay, well, why don't we meet for lunch, so you can convince me of that, okay?"

Sarah was silent, so many things ran through her mind, wanting to push back, wanting to mention Skyler, but also wanting desperately to talk to Devin.

"Sarah?" Devin queried.

"Yeah, I'm here," Sarah said, her tone all Marine.

"Okay, well, stop over thinking the invitation and just accept it, will ya?" Devin said, smiling as she did.

She heard Sarah's chuckle on the other end. "Oorah," Sarah said, her way of accepting that Devin knew her well enough to know what she'd been thinking.

They met at a local restaurant later that day. Devin could see that Sarah was very nervous, as they said their hellos and chatted. Sarah's hands were shaking and she kept clasping them together, releasing them when she saw Devin looking at them. Finally, Devin couldn't take anymore, she placed her hands over Sarah's as she sat forward.

"Relax," Devin said, her voice soothing.

Sarah swallowed visibly and nodded her head. "Sorry."

"Sarah, I'm not here to vilify you, okay?" Devin told her. "I just want to see how you are."

Sarah looked back at her then shrugged,. "I'm fine," she said, her tone overly casual. "It wasn't what Amy thought."

Devin looked Sarah right in the eyes. "You know that bullshit story probably worked on the Navy doctor, but please don't try to sell that one to me."

Sarah looked surprised for a moment, then pressed her lips together. "Not good at lying to you, am I?"

"Nope," Devin said with a smile, "never have been." Then she put her hand over Sarah's again. "What happened?"

Sarah sat back in her chair, her focus turned inward. "I just couldn't get a handle on things," she said, shaking her head.

"What things?" Devin asked, as the waitress came over to hand them menus.

When the waitress left again, Sarah said, "Things, you know, being out, you being with someone else, just stuff."

Devin nodded taking in the comment about her.

"I guess I just didn't know how to handle it," Sarah said, sounding defeated.

"Okay, but you have to deal with things, Sarah," Devin said, her voice soft, "or you're going to end up in that dark place again."

"I know," Sarah said, nodding.

"Will you let me help?" Devin asked.

"How's your girlfriend going to like that?" Sarah asked, her tone doubtful.

"Skyler knows all about this."

"Great," Sarah said, her tone defeated as she shook her head.

"Sarah, Skyler is the one that suggested I help you," Devin said, wanting to defend Skyler's motives in this situation.

"Seriously?" Sarah said, looking shocked.

"Yeah," Devin said, "she's been through a lot herself."

Sarah looked like she was considering that information. "Like what?"

Devin looked back at Sarah hesitating, not sure if she should share Skyler's tragedy, but in the end she figured it might help in some way.

"She lost two members of her unit in a helicopter crash in Iraq."

"Jesus..." Sarah muttered, "that's rough."

"Yeah and I can tell you she still needs to deal with some stuff from it, but she's pushing forward."

Sarah nodded, looking affected. "So you're saying that I should buck it up, huh?"

"No," Devin said, shaking her head. "I'm just saying that my girlfriend understands that things get hard for people and she supports me helping you through this."

Sarah drew in a deep breath, blowing it out slowly as she nodded, reconciling in her head that the person she'd considered an enemy was not quite the bad guy she'd thought.

The rest of their lunch together was spent talking about other things. Devin knew that Sarah wasn't ready to talk about what issues she needed to deal with and she'd learned from Skyler how not to push someone.

That night Devin told Skyler about the lunch.

"So you think she's going to let you help?" Skyler said.

"I think so, yeah."

Skyler nodded. "That's good."

"Yeah."

They moved on to other topics then. Skyler told her about a training conference she was being sent to in the next week or so, up in Sacramento.

"How long will you be gone?" Devin asked.

"Two weeks," Skyler said. "They have us doing some field training with some of the other units up there."

Devin nodded understanding. She knew she'd been lucky lately that her job had kept her in Los Angeles. She was nearly finished with the job for the LAPD, then she'd have to start looking at other job offers. Some of those offers were in Washington, D.C. which would mean time outside of LA and also away from Skyler. Devin wasn't sure how she felt about that, usually she wasn't that attached to someone she was dating. Skyler was different for her; she had been since the first day they'd met. She also decided she wasn't going to worry about where her next job would be until she had to do just that.

When Skyler left a week later, it didn't take long till Devin felt like she'd go nuts trying to fill her days and evenings with stuff to do to keep from missing Skyler. She found herself driving to Camp Pendleton a lot, where Sarah was based. She spent a lot of time just hanging out with her in Oceanside. Often they'd sit in a coffee shop and just talk. Little by little Sarah was talking about things that were bothering her.

One such occasion they were talking about how coming out had affected her and Devin was fairly sure she'd hit on a significant factor in Sarah's suicide attempt.

"My dad disowned me," Sarah said after describing how her friends had taken the news.

She said it in an off-handed manner. Anyone else wouldn't have likely picked up on the hidden meaning behind those words. However, Devin knew that Sarah's father was the reason she'd become a Marine, because her dad had been one. Sarah had worked her whole life to earn her father's approval. Now to have her father disown her because of her sexual orientation, it was the worst possible thing that could have happened as a result of Sarah coming out.

"Sarah…" Devin said, reaching out to cover Sarah's hand with hers, "I'm sorry, that's… that's lousy."

Sarah blinked a couple of times, still surprised that Devin even cared, but also happy that someone understood what her father's abandonment really meant.

"He's the reason I'm a Marine," Sarah said, shaking her head.

"I know," Devin said, nodding, "but maybe it's time to worry less about him and worry more about yourself."

"What do you mean?"

"I mean, you've spent your life trying to be what he wanted you to be, maybe it's time to just be you," Devin said, her voice gentler on the last part.

Sarah stared back at her, looking shocked by the suggestion.

"I don't even know if I'd know how," Sarah said, her face showing the conflict going on inside her.

"Maybe you just need to take some time to think about what you really want," Devin said.

Sarah gave a short laugh. "You mean instead of doing what I'm expected to do?"

"Exactly," Devin said, nodding her head.

Sarah looked like she was really considering the idea and it shocked Devin that it seemed like Sarah had never stopped to consider what exactly *she* wanted. It was sad.

Devin talked to Skyler that night on the phone about it. She filled Skyler in about what she and Sarah had been talking about and how Sarah's family had been growing up. Skyler made a couple of comments, but didn't really talk a lot. Devin would realize later that she should have picked up on this, but didn't at the time.

The night Skyler got back from Sacramento, Devin was caught in traffic on Highway 5 trying to get back to LA from Camp Pendleton. She wasn't home when Skyler got in, but she'd texted to say that she was stuck behind a jackknifed big rig on the freeway and she'd be home as soon as she could.

By the time a much frazzled Devin walked through her front door, Skyler was already in bed. Walking into the bedroom, Devin noted that Skyler had unpacked, but hadn't put her duffle bag away, she wondered about that.

Walking over to the bed, she leaned down and kissed Skyler softly on the lips. Skyler stirred opening her eyes.

"Hi," Devin said, smiling.

"Hi," Skyler echoed tiredly.

"I'm going to take a quick shower and then I'll be in, okay?"

"'Kay," Skyler said, moving to turn over on her side.

By the time Devin crawled into bed, Skyler was asleep again. For the first time in a very long time, Skyler didn't reach out and pull her close when she climbed into bed. At the time, Devin was too tired to notice the subtle change.

The next day Skyler was up and gone before Devin even stirred. Later in the day, Skyler called Devin on her cell. Devin picked up, answering absently. She was working on a line of code in a program she was writing so she was distracted.

She tuned in to hear Skyler saying, "... so I'm going to head there tonight."

"Head where? I'm sorry," Devin said, realizing that she'd missed something.

"Sebo is losing his shit," Skyler said, her tone pointedly patient, "so I'm going to head there tonight."

"Wait, head where?" Devin said. "Home? You're going home?" she asked, shocked.

Skyler had patently refused to go home to help her brother with his legal woes for months, and now she was going, just like that? This was yet another time when Devin's senses should have told her something was amiss, but they failed her again.

"Yeah," Skyler said, her tone nonchalant, "my parents can't handle it, so I'm going to go see what I can do."

"Okay…" Devin said, "well, that's probably good," she continued, trying to rally a supportive attitude. "I'm sure you'll be of a lot of help to him if you put your charm to it," she said then, smiling.

Skyler chuckled. "Yeah, we'll see about that," she said doubtfully.

"So, what time do you need me to take you to the airport?" Devin asked, glancing at her watch, it was already three in the afternoon, where had the time gone?

"Nah," Skyler said, "I'm just gonna fly out of Burbank, one of the guys will fly me over."

"You already packed?" Devin asked, shocked, remembering the duffle bag being out the night before.

"Yeah, I meant to tell you last night," Skyler said, "but…"

"I know," Devin said, biting her lip, "I got in really late."

"Yeah," Skyler said flatly. "So…"

"Okay," Devin said, pushing her disappointment down, thinking that the last thing Skyler needed right now was a whiney girlfriend. "I guess I'll see you when you get back?"

"Yeah," Skyler said.

"How long are you gonna be gone?" Devin asked, realizing they hadn't even talked about it at that point.

"Dunno," Skyler said, "maybe a couple days, maybe three…"

"Okay," Devin said. "Well, call me to let me know you got on, okay, will ya?"

"Of course," Skyler said.

"Okay," Devin said, feeling a tugging at her heart, "I love you."

"Love you," Skyler said, her tone brisk. "Gotta go babe, we're getting a call out. I'll call you tonight."

"Okay, fly safe." Devin said, quickly before Skyler ran off.

"You got it," Skyler said, then hung up a moment later.

Devin didn't hear from Skyler that night, but she got a quick text that said her flight had been delayed in Dallas. In the end Skyler got to Baton Rouge and to her hotel almost a full twenty-four hours after she'd left; what should have been a fourteen hour trip. She'd texted Devin when she'd arrived in Baton Rouge at five-thirty PM, she was exhausted so she fell into her hotel bed happily.

By the next morning, she woke generally refreshed and made her way to her family home. She drove a rental car, but she'd decided to splurge on a nicer car for herself. She drove a Corvette Stingray convertible, enjoying the drive, even though she knew she'd attract attention with the car, especially since it was red. It was the fastest thing she could find that would at least give her the satisfaction of power, with its four hundred sixty horsepower eight-cylinder engine.

Pulling up in front of her parents' home, she couldn't resist revving the engine one last time before turning the car off. She could see people poking their heads out of their houses, and the hood rats in the neighborhood motioning to each other to look at the car. Skyler grinned to herself, knowing she was taking a risk bringing this car to this neighborhood, but she'd purposely bought full insurance for the expensive car, just in case.

Climbing out of the low-slung sports car, she walked to the door. She looked every bit the California girl with her tan and shades on. She wore her customary jeans and combat style boots, she also wore her LAFD t-shirt, with a picture of a helicopter and "Air Operations" on the back, with the "Air Operations" gold wings on the front chest pocket.

She knocked on the door, waiting to see how her family would react to her arrival.

"Who dat?" her mother said, coming to the screen door.

Her mother's look of complete shock irritated Skyler. It wasn't as if the woman hadn't called her constantly for the last two weeks. Even crying a few times when Skyler had refused to come home to help her brother.

"It's me," Skyler said, her tone annoyed.

"Abel!" Bettina Boché yelled. "Look who's hea!" she said, as she opened the screen door to let Skyler into the house.

"What?" Skyler's father, Abel, yelled from the back of the house. "Who hea?"

"Skyla!" Bettina called.

Skyler remembered now why she hadn't had any problems with drill sergeants yelling at her while she'd been in the Army. Her parents yelled all the time.

"Well, come hea girl!" Bettina said, smiling a toothy smile as she held out her arms to her daughter.

Skyler took after her father in height, standing taller than her mother by six full inches. She hugged her mother, noting that her mother seemed to be much slighter than she'd been years before. She realized belatedly that it had been over six years since she'd been home last. The last visit had been enough for her to stay away for as long as she could.

Skyler heard her father lumbering down the hallway, and waited. Abel Boché was a large man, standing a full six foot four with brawn to match. At least that had been the case the last time Skyler had been home. Her father seemed to have deflated a bit over the last six years. He still had his height, even though he seemed shorter due to the stoop he had developed, but he definitely had lost a lot of his brawn. Skyler couldn't control the raise of her eyebrow at the sight of him and her father saw it.

"Wha? I look old?" her father demanded, his voice still booming.

Skyler did her best to suppress her wry grin. "I didn't say a word," she enjoined.

"I know dat look," her father snapped, even so he walked over to look her over.

Skyler straightened her back, her eyes staring right back into her father's, refusing to show any weakness in front of the man. He no longer intimidated her. He'd done his worst the last time she'd been home, she was no longer afraid of him. Her looks told him that.

After a long look, Abel nodded, as if he'd confirmed something to himself.

"So you came home after all, eh?" Abel said, moving to sit in his chair, his tone uninterested.

"I couldn't miss the phone calls I got begging me to do just that," Skyler countered.

Abel snorted dismissively as he used the remote to turn on the TV. Skyler shook her head, reaching into her back pocket for a cigarette and into her front pocket for her lighter. She walked through the house, heading for the backyard, just needing to get away from them for a few minutes. It's where Sebastian found her a half an hour later.

"How long did that take?" Sebastian asked from behind her.

Skyler grinned. "'Bout a minute."

Sebastian walked around to look at her. She was seated in one of the lawn chairs, her phone on her knee blaring out Linkin Park, and a number of cigarette butts on the ground at her feet. The song "What I've Done" was playing and Skyler was singing the words.

The lines that talked about forgetting what others thought of her, and trying to wipe the slate clean, and asking for mercy for what she'd "done" seemed to resonate. Sebastian was pretty sure that his big sister was thinking of her time in Iraq. He didn't know exactly what had happened to her, but he knew she'd nearly been killed and that two people in her crew had been killed. Skyler hadn't come home after the incident, but the military had told them a general story of what had happened.

Sebastian had been sure there was more the Army hadn't told them. He had hurt for his sister during that time. It had hurt him that

148

she hadn't come home, but he knew that their parents had everything to do with that. He knew that their parents were terrible to Skyler, but he'd always looked up to her. She was the toughest, biggest badass he knew, and he'd been so proud to tell his friends that his sister was an Army pilot over fighting the war. The fact that his sister had flown a Black Hawk helicopter was something he was very proud of and bragged about it even now. He hated that he'd lost touch with her.

Now, seeing her sitting in their childhood backyard, where they'd built a fort as kids, it all came back to him, and he realized how much he'd really missed his big sister. The fact that she was likely there to try and save his ass made him feel ashamed. He didn't care if he disappointed their parents. *Fuck them*, he always thought, but disappointing Skyler was a lot easier to handle when she wasn't sitting right there in front of him.

"So…" he said, sitting down across from her, blowing his breath out anxiously.

Skyler looked at her kid brother, he was two years her junior, but she always saw him as much younger. He was a handsome devil, she thought as she always had. He had the blue-green eye color she had, and the darker skin of the Cajun side. His hair, currently bleached blond on top with a long fade, and the sides that were shaved close to his head was his natural reddish brown.

"So…" Skyler mimicked, her grin wry as she waited for him to talk.

She knew he was hoping she'd say something first, but she had no intention of excusing his current situation.

"Don't fuckin do that!" he said, his voice raised, but a grin on his lips.

"Do what?" Skyler asked, leaning back in her chair.

"You know what," he said, giving her a narrowed look. "You're worse than them!"

That made Skyler smile evilly. "Why?"

"'Cause I give a shit what you think, damnit!" he said, glowering at her.

"Then stop doing stupid shit, Sebo," Skyler said.

"Yeah, yeah," he said, rolling his eyes at her.

"Yeah, yeah," Skyler repeated giving him a direct look.

"I fucked up, okay? I know that," Sebastian said.

Skyler nodded, her look saying that she agreed with him.

"But you're here," he said, chewing on the inside of his cheek in tentativeness, "so does that mean you're gonna help me?"

The look in Sebastian's eyes went straight to Skyler's heart, she could see that he was scared, and that he was looking to her to save him. It jabbed at her that she really had abandoned her baby brother with their asshole parents, it really wasn't his fault that they'd always treated her like shit, and him like a king. She'd told herself over the years that he could have done anything else with his life, but she wasn't as sure of that sitting in their backyard in the worst part of town.

Skyler gave him a considering look. "I'm not sure that I'm as influential as our parents think, Sebo," She said honestly.

"But you might be," he said. He sounded like a little boy, with all the hope and trust that came with that.

Skyler grinned. "I don't know," she said.

"But you'll try?" Sebastian asked hopefully.

"I'll try," Skyler said.

Sebastian blessed her with his most winning smile and Skyler couldn't help but roll her eyes and shake her head. The little shit definitely had a way.

"Now, let's go hit the hood with that bad ass car you brought!" he said, smiling brightly.

Skyler laughed at his enthusiasm, moving to stand as Sebastian did the same. She was surprised when she was caught up in a hug.

Sebastian was taller than her by a few inches, so his lips grazed the side of her head as he said, "Thanks sis," quietly and gave her an extra squeeze.

Skyler was surprised when tears sprang to her eyes. She really had missed him. It was hard not to miss him. He was all charm and personality.

They left their parents' home in the Corvette, taking a drive through the neighborhood. Sebastian was hailed by a number of people, some even recognized Skyler, even though she hadn't lived there in years.

"So what ya doin' these days, anyway?" Sebastian asked her.

Skyler grimaced, she hadn't really shared a lot with her family over the years. She figured they didn't care, so she wasn't going to go out of her way to tell them anything. But it was sad that her own brother didn't seem to know what she did for a living now.

"I'm working for LA fire," Skyler said.

"You're a fire fighter?" Sebastian asked shocked.

Skyler laughed, shaking her head. "No, sorry, I work air operations." At his blank look she clarified, "I fly a rescue chopper."

"Oh, oh, I get it!" Sebastian said. "Dat's pretty cool."

"It has its moments."

"Uh-huh," Sebastian murmured. Convinced that she was holding out on him.

"So, what else is goin' on with ya?" Sebastian asked.

Skyler didn't answer right away, then shrugged. "Not too much."

"Is there a girl? Or are there a lot of girls?" Sebastian asked, sounding lecherous.

Skyler chuckled. "Just one at the moment," she said, her features darkening a bit.

"Uh oh," Sebastian said, "problems with that one?"

Skyler blew her breath out. "Just complications," she said non-committally.

"Ah, those," Sebastian said nodding wisely.

"What about you?" Skyler asked, amazed that she was having this conversation with her brother.

"Nah," Sebastian said, "I play it fast and loose these days."

"These days?" Skyler repeated.

"Always," Sebastian said with a devilish grin.

"More like it," Skyler said, laughing.

"So is she hot?"

Skyler handed him her phone. "She's on there."

Sebastian scrolled through the pictures, coming across one with Devin and Skyler.

"Holy shit, Sky, she's definitely hot."

Skyler grinned, nodding. Sebastian continued to scroll through the pictures and came across one of a hot Latina.

"Who's this?" he asked holding up the phone.

Skyler glanced over, at the phone, grinning. "That's Rose," she said, "an ex."

"You don't slouch do ya?" Sebastian said, grinning.

Skyler shrugged shaking her head.

"So how come she didn't come with you?" he asked.

Skyler made a face. "It's complicated right now."

"Complicated?"

"Yeah."

"Wanna talk about it?"

"Wit you?" Skyler said, letting her Cajun accent show for a moment.

"No huh?" Sebastian asked.

"No," Skyler confirmed.

"Okay, okay…" Sebastian said, holding up his hands in surrender, even as he grinned.

It was a nice day, they ended up having lunch at one of Skyler's old hot spots.

Later, back at the hotel, Skyler checked her phone and saw that Devin had called a few times. She knew in her heart of hearts that she was being a coward not talking to Devin about how she was feeling about her time with Sarah. She knew she'd been the one to encourage Devin to help Sarah, through this rough part of her life. And she still agreed with that, she just hadn't known how it would feel knowing they were spending so much time together. It made her wonder if she'd been standing in Devin's way when it came to Sarah. She'd decided that absenting herself from the middle of things would tell the tale.

She dialed Devin's number and got her voicemail, so she just left a brief message.

"Hey, it's me. Spent the day with my brother. Shit is the same here as it always is. Talk to you later." And then she hung up. She knew she was being distant with Devin, but she also knew that she didn't want to look stupid if Devin ended up back with Sarah after all of this. She still had to protect herself too.

That night Sebastian and Skyler went to a local bar and just drank and played pool. It was an easy night. Skyler knew she pushed it on the alcohol, but she made sure she was still okay to drive that night to drop Sebastian off at their parents' house.

The next day was supposed to be Sebastian's first appearance in court. Their parents and a few other relatives were in attendance. The case ended up being continued until the following month, but Skyler took the opportunity to talk to the prosecuting DA, Matt Modela. While her family looked on, Skyler stepped up to the DA.

"Good morning sir," Skyler said, extending her hand to the man, she could easily sense that the man was ex-military by his mannerisms.

The DA gave her a slightly suspicious look, having seen her sitting with the defendant during the case. It was also evident by their similar features that they were related. Slowly he extended his hand to her, his look cautious.

"Skyler Boché," Skyler told him. "Sebastian is my brother."

"I understand," Matt said, nodding his head. "What can I do for you Ms. Boché?"

"I was hoping I could talk to you about my brother's case," Skyler said, moving to stand in what any military person would recognize as an at-ease position.

"I can't really discuss the case, Ms. Boché," Matt said recognizing ex-military in Skyler.

It occurred to him then that he'd read in Sebastian's file that his sister had been a decorated Army pilot. He'd read that Skyler Boché had received the Medal of Honor, no mean fete for a woman in the military. She'd also been awarded a Purple Heart for injuries sustained in a crash. He also remembered thinking that Sebastian hadn't been anything like his sister.

"I understand completely, sir," Skyler said, reaching up to rub the bridge of her nose in agitation, she hated to be in this position. "I was hoping to ask you about the possibility of probation."

Matt looked back at her in mild surprise, but out of respect for her status he was willing to hear her out.

"That's asking for a helluva gift, Ms. Boché," he said, his eyes skipping from Skyler to the faces of her family standing around them. "Under what circumstances?" Matt asked.

Skyler paused, she wanted to be careful here; she wanted to keep Sebastian out of jail, but she wasn't sure if her solution would be enough.

"I work for the Los Angeles Fire Department, Air Operations. I had a chance to talk to my CO earlier this morning. He said he'd be willing to recommend Sebo—Sebastian as a probationary fire fighter with our department."

"That's remarkable," Matt said, impressed that Skyler didn't seem to be trading on her Medal of Honor or her military background, even though he was sure she recognized him as fellow ex-military personnel. "But how do I know he won't just go sell drugs in California?"

"Because I'd beat him senseless if he tried," Skyler practically growled as she shot her brother narrowed look.

Matt had to grin at that statement and he believed Skyler Boché would do just that. He considered his case, and the impact this would possibly have on Sebastian Boché's life.

"You'd be willing to personally vouch for him?" Matt asked her then.

Skyler took a deep breath, her look considering, but then she nodded. "I would sir," she said, her tone respectful.

"I understand you gave a lot to our country," Matt said, his tone equally respectful.

Skyler blinked a couple of times, nodding, her look grave. "Others gave more," she said, her voice tinged with the tears that were in her throat suddenly.

Matt nodded, uttering a, "Hooah," understanding exactly what she meant. He'd lost enough soldiers in his unit during his time in the military.

He extended his hand to Skyler. "Your brother is very lucky to have you backing him up," he told her, nodding his head to her. "I'll petition the judge for two years' probation," he pinned her with a look then, "but if he fucks up on your watch…"

"I'll bring him back to jail myself," Skyler said, her tone no nonsense.

Matt nodded, then moved to pick up his brief case.

He extended his hand to Skyler once again. "Good to meet you soldier," he said, giving her a direct look.

"You too sir, thank you." Skyler answered, returning his look.

Matt's eyes skipped to the Boché family, he was wondering why none of them had spoken. It seemed odd, but he'd talked to the person he was willing to trust. That was enough. With that he walked out of the courtroom.

Sebastian grabbed his sister up in a hug, as the rest of the family let out a collective sigh of relief. Skyler saw that her father was nodding, the look on his face conciliatory, but nowhere near grateful. She shrugged it off; she didn't care if they appreciated what she'd done, or how far out on a ledge she'd gone for Sebastian, she hadn't done it for them.

"We have to go out and celebrate!" Sebastian said as they walked out of the courthouse. "I'm gonna be a fireman!"

It had actually been something he'd wanted to do when he was younger, but it just hadn't ever happened. He'd fallen in with a bad crowd after Skyler had left for the military and before he knew it, he was making easy money selling drugs. The arrest had brought him up short and he'd realized that he was headed down a bad path, he just hadn't been able to figure out how to get out of it. Skyler had saved him.

That night he hailed her as his hero to anyone who would listen. They did some bar hopping, and when they drove into another parking lot, they'd noticed a lot of heads turning. They made a striking pair, Skyler wore all black, including her usual black combat-style boots. Sebastian was also wearing black, the two of them turned heads anyway, but the convertible red Corvette turned heads too.

Inside the bar Skyler and Sebastian had just gotten beers and were leaning with their backs to the bar when a woman approached them. She had long dark hair, and a quite curvy body, easily noticeable in the tight dress she wore.

"Is that your Vette out there?" she asked Sebastian.

Sebastian glanced at Skyler, then nodded his head toward her. "It's my sister's," he told the girl.

The girl looked at Skyler, her look assessing, then she smiled brightly. "That's a seriously hot car," she said, stepping over to stand in front of Skyler, as she reached up to flip her hair over her shoulder provocatively.

Skyler looked back at the girl, her look considering. "I'd like to say I own it, but it's a rental."

"That's okay," the girl replied, licking her lips, "so you're not from here then?"

"Not anymore," Skyler said.

"Where do you live now?"

"In Los Angeles," Skyler said, taking a drink of her beer and glancing at Sebastian who was making 'oh my god!' faces at her from behind the girl.

"Oh, I love California!" the girl exclaimed. "I'm gonna buy you a drink," she said then, moving up close to Skyler.

Skyler held up her beer to indicate that she already had one.

"A shot then," the girl said.

Skyler inclined her head.

"What'll you have?" the girl asked.

"Ladies choice," Skyler replied.

"Tequila then!" the girl said, holding up two fingers to the bartender, who obviously knew her.

"I'm Serena," the girl said then, putting her hand out to Skyler.

"Skyler," Skyler replied, then nodded at her brother. "He's Sebastian."

"Nice to meet you both!" Serena said, as the bartender handed her the shots, he'd added a third shot grinning at Sebastian, who nodded gratefully at the man.

They downed their shots. Just then the DJ changed the song and Pit Bull and Ricky Martin's "Mr. Put it Down" came on.

"I love this song!" Serena squealed, grabbing both of their hands and dragging them toward the dance floor.

Sebastian and Skyler exchanged a look, neither of them believing this situation.

Even so, they found themselves singing along with the song as the three of them danced.

The chorus, "Who has a lifetime, baby? We got the life right now? When you see what I'm planning, you're gonna call me Mr. Put it Down!" was sung with gusto.

After the song ended, the three of them ended up at a table together. There was a lot of talking, and a lot of flirting on Serena's part, primarily with Skyler.

"So how come you left Baton Rouge?" Serena asked Skyler.

"I joined the Army," Skyler said.

"Wow, really?" Serena said, looking impressed.

"She's a pilot," Sebastian put in.

"Really?" Serena asked, her eyes lighting up. "That's awesome!"

Skyler looked over at Sebastian, narrowing her eyes at him. He only laughed, nodding his head.

"She also got the Medal of Honor," he added.

"Sebo!" Skyler hollered.

"Medal of Honor?" Serena queried, looking mystified. "What's that?"

Skyler chuckled, raising an eyebrow at Sebastian.

"The president gave it to her," Sebastian said, "you know, like Obama."

Serena's eyes widened as she looked back over at Skyler. Fortunately, Skyler's phone rang at that moment. She stood up, pulling her phone out, seeing that it was Devin, she walked away from the table.

Picking up the call, as she headed out the door of the club so she could actually hear, she said, "Hey."

"Hi," Devin said, her tone subdued, it put Skyler on alert instantly.

"What's up?" she asked, keeping her voice purposely casual, even as she leaned against the nearest wall, and pulled out a cigarette, lighting it.

"I need to tell you something," Devin said, her tone cautious, "but I need you to hear me out."

On her end Skyler closed her eyes slowly, even as she took a long draw off her cigarette.

"Go ahead," Skyler said when Devin didn't continue.

Skyler heard Devin take a deep breath and blow it out. "Okay, look, Sarah kissed me today," she said, speaking quickly, like saying it fast would make it hurt less.

It didn't hurt less. Skyler narrowed her eyes on her end of the phone.

"Okay," Skyler said after a long pause.

"It wasn't anything," Devin said, "I just wanted to tell you."

"Because it wasn't anything," Skyler said, her tone flat.

"Right," Devin said. "I mean, no, I wanted to tell you, but it wasn't anything, that wasn't why I wanted to tell you."

"Okay," Skyler said flatly again.

On her end Devin was clutching the phone. She wasn't sure what else to say, she didn't want to go on and on with an explanation because that would make it worse, but Skyler wasn't really giving her anything to work with.

"Where are you?" Devin asked, finally, having heard the music when Skyler first answered the phone.

"At a bar," Skyler said, briskly. "Look, I gotta go, I left Sebo with a predator, I gotta go rescue him."

"Okay," Devin said, chuckling at her end, honestly hoping that Skyler was really as lighthearted as she sounded.

"Talk to you later," Skyler said.

"Have fun," Devin said, smiling.

"You got it," Skyler said, then broke the connection.

Staying outside smoking her cigarette, Skyler banged her head against the wall a few times, wanting to hit something. Instead she discarded her cigarette and strode back into the bar and up to the bartender.

"Tequila, double," she ordered.

The man handed her the drink, she downed it and held up her finger for another. When she downed the second shot, she turned to survey the bar. Serena and Sebastian were now on the dance floor, dancing to some pop song.

The song transitioned to Rihanna's "Don't Stop the Music." Skyler pushed herself off the bar and strode to the dance floor and straight over to where Sebastian and Serena were dancing. Sliding her hand around Serena's waist, she pulled her close and began to move with her to the music pumping out of the speakers.

Serena gave herself to the song and slid her hand up Skyler's chest to rest her hand on Skyler's shoulder. The girl could definitely move, Skyler noted, refusing to think beyond what was going on at that moment, letting the alcohol in her veins dull her sense of impropriety or the idea that she was cheating on Devin. As the music transitioned again, Serena's hand slid around Skyler's neck, pulling her head down so she could kiss her. Their lips met and clung for a long minute, Serena's hands were in Skyler's hair, and Skyler was holding onto Serena's waist pulling her closer. After a couple of minutes though, Skyler pulled her head back, breaking the kiss, knowing she couldn't do this.

"I'm sorry," Skyler said, stepping back, nodding her head to Sebastian who had stood by and watched the whole thing. Then she turned and walked away, heading straight out the door to light another cigarette.

Sebastian found her in the parking lot a few minutes later. Without a word he handed her a double shot of tequila which she took and downed gratefully, then he handed her a bottle of beer. Skyler smoked and Sebastian stood by, looking around at the people walking around outside the bar. After about a half hour, Skyler and Sebastian went back inside and Skyler proceeded to get completely drunk.

Sebastian got his chance to drive the Corvette, driving back to their parents' home.

"You gotta come in and sober up, Sky," Sebastian told her.

Skyler nodded, knowing she was far too drunk to drive back to the hotel. They made it into the house, stumbling over furniture and laughing at each other. Shushing each other and getting a good laugh out of that.

"Gotta make you coffee," Sebastian said, leading the way into the kitchen.

"You even know how?" Skyler asked, doubting that fact.

"Sure."

"Do it!"

There was a lot of laughing and spilling of water. Even so, they were both shocked when their father's voice boomed at them from the doorway.

"What da hell is goin' on in hea?!" he bellowed.

Skyler and Sebastian froze like recalcitrant children, then looked at each other and burst into laughter, which only made Abel angrier.

"Shut up!" he bellowed, slamming his fist down on the counter. "Stop dis stupidity! You!" he yelled, jabbing his finger at Skyler. "Comin' hea and causin' such a fuss! Irresponsible, no good—"

"Whoa!" Skyler said, holding her hand up to stop his tirade. "Irresponsible?" she said, suddenly feeling a lot more sober as anger flooded her veins. "You have the fuckin' nerve to call me irresponsible?"

"Don' you cuss at me," Abel spat, his eyes blazing.

"I'll cuss at you old man," Skyler said, her tone dismissive. "I'll say anything I fuckin' want right now."

"Sky…" Sebastian cautioned, but she didn't listen.

"Who was it that saved your boy's ass today? Huh? Who?" Skyler yelled. "It wasn't you, that's for damned sure!"

Abel's mouth worked like he wanted to say something, but he couldn't even form the words.

"What have you ever done that's worth anything, Dad? Huh?" Skyler continued to rage. "Nothin'! That's what, not a fuckin' thing!"

She was actually surprised when his fist caught her in the stomach, and she didn't react fast enough to avoid the hands that grabbed her up like a rag doll and threw her against the counter knocking the wind out of her.

"You low down piece of shit!" her father was screaming. "Come in hea like you da queen, think yer all dat! Well you ain't, you're just a low down disgusting dyke!"

Skyler's anger drove her to her feet and she charged her father, catching him in the midsection and ramming him into the wall behind him. He shoved her away from him, and caught her in the side with his fist. She twisted around, slamming her fist home on his jaw. Abel fell heavily and didn't get back up.

Skyler stood over her father, panting with her fists balled as she watched to see if he'd get back up.

"What's goin' on out hea?" their mother called as she strode down the hallway.

Sebastian grabbed Skyler's hand and dragged her out of the house as they heard their mother wailing and screaming for Abel to get up. Sebastian shoved Skyler into the Corvette and jumped in the driver's seat, starting the car with a roar. Throwing the car into gear he screeched the tires taking off.

They drove for a while, both of them lost in their thoughts. As she started to calm down, Skyler started to feel the pain in her chest. She'd struck the counter at the corner, slamming her ribs into it. She'd known at the time she'd broken at least one rib but the adrenaline had kept her going.

"Need more alcohol," Skyler said.

"What hotel you at?" Sebastian asked.

"Renaissance."

"Nice…" Sebastian murmured as he took a quick left.

They made it to the hotel a few minutes after stopping at a liquor store to buy three bottles of tequila. At the hotel they got drunk and didn't talk about what had happened.

Two days later, Skyler was still consistently drunk and Sebastian was worried about his sister. So much so, that he decided he needed to call someone who knew her best. Picking up her phone while she was in the bathroom, he looked at her contact list for names. He recognized Jams as Skyler's copilot in the Army, he'd heard the name often enough.

Dialing the number on his phone he got up and walked out onto the balcony.

"Yeah?" Jams answered, his tone indicating he had no idea who was calling.

"Is this Jams?" Sebastian asked.

"Yeah…" Jams replied. "Who's this?"

"This is Sebastian Boché, Skyler's brother."

"Holy fuck, where is she?" Jams asked. He'd been worried sick about his best friend, and had been calling her phone constantly, as had Devin. He'd been about to head to Baton Rouge himself.

Sebastian nodded to himself, knowing he'd done the smart thing in calling Jams. "She's here at the Renaissance hotel in Baton Rouge," Sebastian said, "but she's messed up."

"Messed up, how?" Jams asked, his voice taking on a different tone.

"She got into it with our dad a few nights ago," Sebastian said.

"Fuck…" Jams said, knowing how violent Skyler's father was, and also knowing how big the man was too. "Is she okay? I mean, is she hurt?"

"Yeah…" Sebastian said, "…that's the thing, I think she is, but she won't do anything about it."

"Yeah, that sounds like Sky," Jams said, sighing. "Okay, we'll be on a plane tonight."

"We?" Sebastian queried.

"Her girlfriend, Devin, will remove my head if I don't tell her, she's been worried sick about her."

"Okay," Sebastian said, nodding, remembering that Skyler had mentioned things being complicated.

Chapter 7

Devin paced in the airport as they waited for their plane. They'd managed to secure a flight with only one stop, which got them to Baton Rouge in just over five hours. The commanding officer for Air Operations had a connection with United Airlines and had managed to secure them seats on short notice. He'd told Jams that he was under no circumstances to come back without his pilot. Jams thanked the CO profusely.

Once on the plane, Devin could not relax. She needed to know that Skyler was okay, but she had no way of knowing that. Jams had told her that Skyler had gotten into a fight with her father, and that Sebastian thought she was hurt, but wouldn't get medical attention. That's all they knew.

"I still can't believe this," Devin said to Jams.

"Which part?" Jams asked, glancing over at her.

"Her father actually struck her?"

"That's what it sounds like," Jams said, shrugging nonchalantly. "It's not the first time, Devin."

"What do you mean?"

"I mean, it isn't the first time Skyler and her father have come to blows."

"They've fought before, physically?"

"Oh yeah," Jams said. "They got into a major fight last time she was home. That's why she hasn't been home in a long time."

Devin shook her head, unable to comprehend that level of violence; especially not with your own child. Devin was pretty sure she didn't want to meet Skyler's parents.

They talked about other things then, but Devin still couldn't fathom what kind of man would strike his own daughter. Sure her parents were somewhat disappointed in her choice of career, but they'd never even considered spankings let alone real physical violence.

It was eleven-thirty PM by the time their plane landed in Baton Rouge. They got a rental car and used the GPS on Devin's phone to locate the hotel. Jams called Sebastian and got the room number from him when they arrived.

Sebastian opened the door to Skyler's hotel room, looking both relieved and anxious at the same time.

"You're Jams?" Sebastian asked, extending his hand to the other man.

"Yeah," Jams replied, taking Sebastian's proffered hand and shaking it firmly.

Sebastian's eyes fell on Devin then. "And you're Devin."

"Yes."

She was amazed at how much Sebastian looked like Skyler; his eyes were the same color, and although he had partly blond hair, he had the same facial features that Skyler did. He was a very handsome man.

"Come on in," Sebastian said, moving out of their way to allow them inside. "She's in there," Sebastian said, motioning to the bedroom door.

Jams nodded, glancing at Devin.

Devin walked to the door, opening it quietly and peering inside. She saw Skyler lying face down on the bed, one tanned arm hanging over the end of the bed. And spotted a number of empty beer bottles as well as a couple of tequila bottles on the nightstand and the floor.

"Jesus…" Jams breathed, taking in the scene.

Sebastian hovered at the door, as Devin and Jams stepped inside the room.

Devin walked toward the bed, she noted a couple of large dark bruises on Skyler's arm and left shoulder. She grimaced at the sight of them, afraid of what else she'd see in the next few minutes.

"Skyler…" she whispered softly, reaching out to touch Skyler's back gently.

When Skyler didn't even stir, Devin repeated her name, louder this time.

Skyler moved then, making a groaning noise deep in her throat. Devin saw one blue-green eye open then narrow, like Skyler was trying to figure out if she was seeing things. Skyler then lifted her head off the bed, with a look of utter confusion on her face.

"Wat you doin' hea?" she asked, her Cajun accent thick, her voice both harsh and gravelly.

"We were worried about you," Devin said, moving to kneel next to the bed, so she could see Skyler more closely.

Skyler made a dismissive sound. "Why?"

"We haven't heard from you in two days," Jams put in, as he stepped up behind where Devin knelt.

Skyler closed her eyes, like Jams voice had been too painful on her ears.

"'Kay," she answered simply.

Skyler then dropped her head to the bed again, and it was obvious she was unconscious again.

Jams blew his breath out. "Well that got us nowhere," he said, attempting to be jovial.

Jams put his hand out to help Devin up, then moved to carefully turn Skyler over to her back.

Devin gasped at the dark bruise that was evident above the neck-line of the tank top Skyler wore. Jams grimaced at the sight, then reached over and carefully gathered the bottom of the tank top to lift it so he could see her rib area.

"Damnit," he muttered, "she's got at least one broken rib, God knows how much internal bleeding. We need to get her to a hospital, *now*." He reached down and carefully scooped his partner up in his arms. "Let's go," he said, motioning with his head to the door.

Within the hour they were at the hospital. It took another four hours until anyone came out to talk to them. They'd been told that she had not regained consciousness. Jams wasn't sure if it was the alcohol or something much worse so he paced the entire time they waited for the doctor. When the doctor walked out from the double doors he looked around, the three walked over to him immediately.

"You're here for Skyler Boché?" the doctor asked.

"Yes," Jams said.

"Are you family?" he asked.

"I'm her brother," Sebastian said, his tone brooking no argument.

The doctor nodded. "Ms. Boché, while being very intoxicated, is also suffering from two cracked ribs and a severe contusion to her sternum. While not life-threatening, she is going to be in a lot of pain for a while. We noticed on the X-rays that there are a lot of healed fractures to her chest area," the doctor said, his tone taking on a suspicious note. "Is Ms. Boché in an abusive relationship?"

Jams gave a short snort of laughter. "Only if you count an Army helicopter, doc," he said. "We were in a crash in Iraq, she broke a number of ribs, and punctured a lung, all kinds of fun stuff." His tone indicated that he was not joking.

"Oh," the doctor said, nodding, "that would explain the previous injuries, thank you." Then he looked at the three of them. "Did she have another crash?" he asked pointedly.

All three of them hesitated, not sure how to answer that question.

"I think you should probably ask her," Jams said, looking to Sebastian for confirmation. Sebastian nodded in agreement.

"Alright then," the doctor said nodding.

"Can we see her?" Devin asked then.

"Certainly, come this way," the doctor said, leading them back into the treatment area.

Skyler was partially lying, partially sitting up in a hospital bed, but her eyes were closed. She was hooked up to an IV. Devin could see all the bruising on Skyler clearly now and it scared her. She had to blink back the tears that threatened to over-flow at the sight of the woman she loved in such bad shape.

She shook her head as she moved to stand near Skyler's head, reaching down to take Skyler's hand. Then she looked over at Sebastian, her face showing the rage she was feeling.

"How could your father do this?" Devin asked, her tone accusing.

Sebastian looked back at her, surprised by the woman's ire, but happy that his sister had someone that seemed to be willing to champion her.

Sebastian shook his head solemnly, then shrugged in futility. "He always has."

Devin's eyes widened as the impact of that statement hit her.

"Always?" Devin repeated.

"Yep," Sebastian said, his eyes on Skyler.

"Even as a child?" Devin clarified.

Sebastian nodded, looking at Jams to see that the other man looked just as surprised as Devin did. In truth, Jams had long suspected that Skyler had been abused as a kid, but she'd never really said much about it.

"Did he hit you?" Devin asked then.

"No," Sebastian said, his tone flat, his face reflecting shame. "Just her," he said, gesturing to Skyler.

"Why?" Devin asked, almost hysterical.

Sebastian shook his head. "Skyler was always different," he said, his look pained. "She never acted like a regular girl, always hanging out with us guys. She didn't play with dolls, she didn't put on makeup or heels…" His voice trailed off, as his gaze fell on his big sister again. "He hates that about her." Then he shrugged. "That's why she joined the Army the minute she turned eighteen."

Devin blinked repeatedly, shaking her head as she did her best to understand. She knew there was a lot of hate in the world, but she'd never seen it so closely as she was seeing it at that moment.

"He should be shot," Jams stated in the silence that followed Sebastian's accounts.

Devin nodded, agreeing with Jams whole heartedly.

"We could tell the doctor who did it," Sebastian said quietly.

Devin and Jams both looked at him, then looked at each other.

"She'd probably kill us," Jams said.

"Maybe," Devin said, not looking too worried about the prospect.

"Should we take that chance?" Jams asked, looking at Devin then at Sebastian. "Isn't it up to her?" Jams added.

"Is it?" Devin asked.

"Yeah, it is," Skyler answered, surprising them all.

"Skyler!" Devin exclaimed, smiling down at her. "I just meant—" she began.

"I know what you meant," Skyler said, her tone reproving, even as she moved to sit up.

"Don't move too much," Devin said, moving to try and help Skyler.

Skyler held up her hands in a warding off gesture. "I got it," she said sharply.

"Easy…" Jams said to Skyler, his tone cautionary.

Skyler shot him a narrowed look, then blew her breath out, shaking her head.

"Sorry," she said to Devin.

Devin only nodded, stepping back and looking away to hide the tears in her eyes.

Skyler closed her eyes, pushing back the irritation she was feeling. She didn't like that they'd been discussing her like she was a child to be managed. And Devin's comment had ignited her temper. She hadn't meant to lash out like that, but she felt like her emotions were all right there on the surface. She desperately tried to reign in her anger, and calm down. Flexing her arm, she felt the IV shift and she looked up at the IV bag.

"What are they giving me?" she asked no one in particular.

"Uh," Jams stammered, "not sure."

"Can you find out?" Skyler asked.

"Sure," Jams said, his tone of voice a little cautious.

Jams left the room and came back with the doctor in tow a couple of minutes later. The doctor smiled at Skyler.

"Ms. Boché," he began, his voice instructive, which only served to irritate Skyler more, "you have—"

"Cracked ribs," Skyler said, cutting the doctor off, "I know."

"How…" Devin asked, looking over at Skyler.

Skyler shrugged. "Felt 'em break," she said simply.

The doctor looked perplexed for a moment, then he got back on track.

"I've ordered pain meds for you, but—"

"There's nothing you can do for me," Skyler interrupted again. "And you can cancel the meds."

"Ms. Boché…" the doctor began, his tone chiding.

"I've had worse, doc, and didn't have pain meds," Skyler snapped. "And you can get this thing out of my arm too," she said, holding up the arm with the IV in it.

When the doctor hesitated, Skyler canted her head. "You do it or I'll do it, doc, take your pick."

"I'll send a nurse in," the doctor said and made a hasty retreat.

"Think that's a good idea?" Jams asked Skyler.

"I think it's my choice," Skyler said, evenly.

Jams shifted his stance, indicating that he thought she was being unreasonable, but he didn't say anything else.

When the nurse came in and took out the IV, Skyler asked her where her clothes had ended up. The nurse gave her a long look, but had already apparently heard about the difficult patient, so she showed Skyler the bag with her clothes in them.

"Thanks," Skyler said, as she moved to get up out of the bed.

"What are you doing?" Jams asked, even as he moved to steady her when she shifted uncomfortably.

"Leaving," Skyler said simply as she reached for the bag.

"I don't think so," Jams said, moving to block Skyler from reaching her clothes.

Skyler's chin came up, her eyes challenging.

"You can give me that look all day long," Jams said, moving to stand with his legs wide apart, his arms crossed in front of his chest, "but till the doc signs you out, you're not going anywhere."

They had a two-minute stand-off, where the only sound in the room was the ticking of the clock on the wall. Finally, Skyler threw up her hands, leaning back against the bed.

"Fine!" she exclaimed. "But get that doctor back in here now."

Jams narrowed his eyes at Skyler, not liking the way she was acting, and definitely not liking the fact that she was choosing to stay in pain.

Skyler looked back at him, her look defiant.

Jams made an annoyed sound in the back of his throat, shaking his head and muttering as he walked toward the door.

"Watch her!" he growled to Sebastian.

Sebastian had watched the scene before him in fascination. He knew his big sister was tough, but he'd never really seen her in action before. He knew that she was probably being stupid wanting to leave the hospital, but he couldn't help but feel awed at the way she handled herself. *Big sis is a baller!* he thought to himself. He also had to respect that Jams was trying to do what was right for Skyler, and wasn't afraid to stop her or challenge her. It was an interesting dynamic.

Sebastian wasn't sure how he felt about Devin though. He appreciated that she was concerned for Skyler, and he hadn't liked the way Skyler had treated her. He just didn't really have a good read on her yet.

Within an hour, Skyler had signed herself out of the hospital. "AMA" the doctor had insisted. "Against Medical Advice," Skyler had explained, followed by a, "yeah, yeah, give me the damned paper, I'll sign it."

The four of them went back to the hotel and Skyler went to take a shower, while the rest of them sat around in the living room area.

"Is she always like that?" Sebastian asked Jams.

"You mean, a pain in my ass?" Jams replied, with a sly smile.

"Yeah, that," Sebastian said, grinning.

"Not always," Jams said, sitting back in his chair and drinking a beer. "She's usually pretty mellow. She doesn't like hospitals, never has, and I'm betting she's pissed that we're all here to witness her low."

Devin looked over at Jams, she hadn't realized that was a possibility, but it made sense. Skyler was usually so confident and self-sufficient, able to take care of herself. Now she was hurt and weak, and had given in to her demons and drank herself silly.

Moving to stand, Devin looked over at Jams, who was watching her. "I'm going to go check on her," she said.

Jams nodded, his eyes tracking her, his look concerned.

"That's not good," Jams muttered.

"What's not?" Sebastian asked.

"Devin's never seen her like this," Jams said, "she's seen some of it, but not this much at a time."

"What do you mean?" Sebastian asked, more and more curious about his sister.

Jams blew his breath out, taking a drink of his beer, then looked over at Sebastian.

"Sky's been real different since Iraq," he said. "She has highs, and she has lows, and sometimes the lows are just brutal. This is one of those times."

Sebastian nodded. "And you don't think Devin can handle them?"

Jams thought about it for a minute, a slow smile spreading on his lips. "I think if anyone can handle them, it's Devin. I just hope it's enough."

Sebastian looked back at Jams for a long minute, then asked the question he'd been thinking for years now. "The Army didn't tell us everything about that crash, did they?" he asked, his tone both earnest and cautious.

Jams shook his head, his look pained.

Sebastian nodded, pressing his lips together in resignation, then looked back at Jams. "And you're not going to tell me either, are you?"

Jams shook his head. "Nope," he said, "it's not my story to tell."

Sebastian drew a deep breath through his nose, then nodded again. Part of him wanted to know what had really happened, but part of him was afraid that it would hurt too much to hear it.

Devin walked into the bedroom and saw Skyler sitting on the bed, she still wore the clothes she'd come back from the hospital in, and in her hand was a lit cigarette. Skyler was sitting with a wide stance, her elbows on her knees, her head bowed. Devin stood watching her for a while, seeing that her hands were shaking when she lifted the cigarette to her mouth. While she watched, Skyler smoked a cigarette and then lit another.

"I thought you were going to take a shower," Devin said moving to sit next to Skyler on the bed.

Skyler didn't look at her, but grinned. "I am," she said simply.

Devin nodded, canting her head to the side. "Is this a smoking room?" she asked, noting that Skyler was using a glass as an ashtray.

Skyler gave a short laugh. "It is now," she said.

Devin laughed softly. They were both silent for a few minutes.

It was Skyler that spoke first. "When you said 'we were worried,'" she said her tone hesitant, "who did you mean?"

Devin was surprised by the question, and actually thought Skyler might be joking, but then she noticed that one of Skyler's knees was bouncing, a sign that she was agitated. Devin also noticed that Skyler's right thumb was rubbing the palm of her left hand, another sign of distress.

"I meant Jams and me," Devin said, her voice soft.

Skyler didn't respond, only nodding her head, taking another deep drag on her cigarette.

"Who did you think I meant, Sky?" Devin asked gently.

Skyler shook her head, her knee still bouncing, her thumb still moving in her palm.

Devin moved to sit on the floor to get under Skyler's gaze. Skyler's light blue-green eyes met hers, and Devin could feel the despair clearly displayed there.

"Oh, Skyler…" Devin said, her voice a sad whisper, "you thought I meant Sarah and me, didn't you?"

Again, Skyler hesitated, but finally nodded again.

"Oh babe…" Devin said, reaching out to touch Skyler's knee, "I'm with you, I love you."

Skyler looked back at her, her eyes searching Devin's, then she pressed her lips together. "Are you sure that's the best idea?"

"What?" Devin asked, not sure she was following Skyler's thoughts.

"Being with me, staying with me," Skyler said her tone serious. "Is it worth it?"

"Yes it's worth it," Devin said, her tone sharper than she'd meant it to be. "You're worth it," she clarified, her voice softer.

"Why?" Skyler countered her look skeptical.

"What makes you think you're not worth it, Skyler?" Devin asked, turning it around on her.

Skyler shrugged. "That shit at the hospital, all of this, I'm a fuckin' train wreck!"

"You're a human being, Skyler," Devin said, her look entreating. "You've been through so much in your life, more than I even knew, but you're here, you're still strong. You're pushing through."

Skyler let out a short humorless laugh. "Yeah," she said, her tone filled with self-loathing, "that's me."

"Skyler, I couldn't even begin to deal with the things you've dealt with and still be here."

"I didn't always want to stay here," Skyler said, her voice breaking on the last word.

Devin was shocked, so much so that it took her a minute to assimilate that information.

"That's why you wanted me to help Sarah..." she said, her voice trailing off as Skyler nodded.

Skyler let out another short laugh. "I had no idea how it would feel seeing you doing it," she said, her voice quiet.

"Oh, Sky…." Devin said, her face reflecting the pain she saw in Skyler's eyes, "why didn't you say something?"

Skyler shrugged, going back to rubbing her palm with her thumb. "I figured if you were meant to be with her, that's how it would go."

"So when I called you the other night and told you she kissed me…" Devin filled in. "Oh, Skyler, I told you that it meant nothing."

Skyler nodded, agreeing that Devin had said that, but it was evident that she hadn't believed that for a minute.

Devin blew her breath out, shaking her head.

They were both silent again for a little while.

"So what ended up happening with your brother's case?" Devin asked, trying to steer their conversation to safer ground.

Skyler grinned, as she lit another cigarette. "I managed to get him probation."

"How the hell did you manage that?" Devin asked shocked.

Skyler chuckled. "Got our CO to recommend Sebo for a probationary fire fighter position with the LAFD."

"Wow," Devin said, "how many strings did you have to pull to make that happen?"

"A whole helluva a lot," Skyler said.

"So, he's moving to LA?" Devin asked.

"Looks like."

Skyler moved, wincing in pain when she did. Shaking her head, she made a disgusted noise in her throat.

"I don't know what the fuck I thought I was doing coming back here," she said.

"You came to help your brother," Devin said,

Skyler snickered. "Right, yeah."

Devin looked at her for a long moment. "Didn't you?"

Skyler curled her lips, dropping her head.

Devin looked at her, puzzled. "Then…" she began, a thought occurring to her, "you were running."

Skyler rolled her eyes.

"Jesus, Sky…" Devin said, shaking her head again.

Moving to lean up on her knees, Devin took Skyler's face in her hands, kissing her lips softly. "Let's take that shower now."

Four hours later, Devin woke to realize that Skyler wasn't still in bed. Lying in the darkness she could hear voices in the living room area. Getting up, Devin pulled on some clothes and walked out of the bedroom. Skyler was sitting on the couch, her back to the arm of the couch, her legs stretched out. Sebastian and Jams were in the two chairs. All three were drinking beers, they were laughing about something.

Skyler glanced over seeing Devin standing in the doorway to the bedroom, she held out her hand to her. Devin walked over, moving to sit next to Skyler on the couch, perching on the edge. Skyler's arm encircled her waist.

"I lost ya," Devin said with a grin.

"Sorry," Skyler said, "couldn't sleep."

Devin nodded, noting that Skyler looked tired, but not wanting to spoil their fragile truce. It bothered Devin that their relationship had become so tenuous.

Earlier in the evening she'd been surprised by some of the things that Skyler had admitted. It had never occurred to her that the reason Skyler had been so supportive of her helping Sarah was because she'd been in that state of mind at one point. It made sense, Devin realized, but she just hadn't thought that Skyler had that in her; she seemed like such a survivor. Sometimes looks could be deceiving. It was something that made Devin more aware of how much she didn't know about Skyler. It also made her more determined to help this woman through anything she was willing to share.

Sebastian watched Skyler and Devin as they all talked. He noticed that Devin's hand was stroking Skyler's arm that was wrapped around her waist. Glancing at his sister, he saw the fond smile she had on her face. There was a very definite connection between his sister and Devin. He sincerely hoped that Jams was right about Devin and that she could really handle Skyler's demons. Sebastian had realized earlier that night that Skyler wasn't quite as invincible as he'd always pictured her. In a way it scared him, but it also made him glad that he would soon be in the same city as his sister, so he might get a chance to get know this older, wiser and possibly more damaged Skyler.

Three days later, the group arrived back in LA. Jams' girlfriend picked him up at the airport. Devin had hired a car to take Skyler and Sebastian back to her house.

"Now, don't get excited," Skyler told Sebastian as they neared Devin's house, "this isn't my place. It's Devin's, and she's been kind enough to let you stay with her."

"Us," Devin put in.

"Us," Skyler corrected, grinning.

Regardless of the warning, Sebastian was bowled over by Devin's house. He walked around the place looking absolutely stunned.

"This is crazy!" he kept saying.

An hour after they'd gotten home, Sebastian found Skyler sitting in the backyard smoking. He walked over and sat down in the chair next to her.

"Nice crib," he said, grinning.

"Devin's, not mine," Skyler said, not for the first time in the last hour.

"She makes bank, huh?" Sebastian said.

Skyler grinned. "She makes pretty good money, yes," she said, her tone indulgent.

"And you're tappin' that!" Sebastian said, his grin wide.

Skyler gave him a narrowed look. "Watch it."

Sebastian laughed. "Didn't mean nothin' sis, chill!" Then he grinned widely. "It's the pilot thing, right?"

"Huh?" Skyler countered, unable to follow his erratic thought processes.

"You used the pilot thing to bag her, right?" Sebastian asked.

Skyler chuckled, shaking her head. "She pursued me, actually."

"Whoa…" Sebastian said, his look impressed. "So baller sis!"

185

Skyler shook her head, rolling her eyes.

"Speaking of the 'pilot thing,'" Skyler said, lighting another cigarette, "you wanna do a ride along with us tomorrow?"

"In the helicopter?" Sebastian asked, sounding like a little boy suddenly. His eyes lit up excitedly. "Hell ya!"

Skyler laughed. "Okay."

That night they took a short drive down to a local restaurant called Moonshadows Malibu. They were seated out on the patio that overlooked the ocean.

"I could get used to this," Sebastian said expansively.

"Don't," Skyler said, grinning, "probies don't make that much."

"Damn!" Sebastian said grinning too.

"Sebo's going in with me tomorrow," Skyler told Devin.

"Oh, that should be fun," Devin said, smiling. "Skyler's an awesome pilot," she told Sebastian.

"Yeah, yeah," Skyler said, waving her hand dismissively.

"Did she tell you that she saved my life?" Devin asked Sebastian, not willing to let Skyler dismiss her talent that easily.

"Wait, what?" Sebastian said, looking over at Skyler.

Skyler shrugged. "I did my job."

"Right!" Devin said, shaking her head. "She rescued me from my car that was about to go over the edge of a cliff in a mudslide."

"Whoa…" Sebastian said, his voice sounding awed. "You did that?" he asked, looking back at his sister.

"Technically, Jerry rescued you," Skyler said, giving Devin a pointed look.

"Right, you just flew the helicopter," Devin said, her tone acerbic.

Skyler grinned, shaking her head. "That's what they pay me to do."

"Yeah, and you got into trouble for it," Devin said, not wanting Skyler to shrug off such an amazing thing that she'd done.

Skyler didn't answer, just shook her head, her eyes looking out over the ocean.

They moved on to other topics then, but Sebastian didn't forget about it. He asked Skyler about the next day.

The morning started off with Sebastian whistling appreciatively at Skyler's car. He could tell it was his sister's pride and joy.

"This is hot," Sebastian said, as they got into the car.

Skyler grinned. "I love it."

"It's fast, ain't it?" Sebastian asked, his eyes sparkling.

"Oh yeah," Skyler said, proving it by punching it when they got on the open road.

"Wooo!" Sebastian crowed joyously.

Linkin Park played from the speakers, the album Minutes to Midnight was playing. As the song "What I've Done" ended, the next song, "Hands Held High" came on. Sebastian, so much like his sister without even knowing it, reached over to turn the song up.

"I always thought of you when I heard this song," he told Skyler.

Skyler looked over at her brother, surprised by the statement, but nodded as she tuned into the lyrics. The song itself was a kind of rock rap song. The words talked about how the singer wanted people to stand up to the government for sending people to war. Lines that talked about this war being basically the same as the rest, as rich people sent the poor people off to fight their battles for them. It was a definite statement on how the Iraq war seemed to be about nothing other than making people rich; those who weren't the ones doing the fighting or the dying.

It was listening to that song that Skyler realized that her time in Iraq hadn't just affected her and her crew. It had affected her family, at the very least her brother; it was something to think about.

When the song ended, Skyler turned the stereo back down.

"That song, huh?" she asked.

Sebastian nodded his head, his look serious.

Skyler looked over at him, her look apologetic. "I'm sorry," she said simply.

Sebastian shrugged. "It's cool," he said, "I was always proud of you. But when that crash happened..." he said, his voice trailing off as he shook his head. "First they told us your helicopter had crashed, then they said you were missing, then they told us you were back, but hurt. It was just really confusing."

Skyler took a deep breath, blowing it out slowly as she nodded.

Sebastian looked over at his sister, seeing that talking about it was bothering her. He could see that there was a sheen of tears in her eyes, he felt bad that he had caused that.

"But you're here, and you're good," Sebastian said, trying to be positive.

The rest of the ride to the airport was achieved in mostly silence.

That day during his ride along, Sebastian got to see his sister in action, and he couldn't help but be impressed. When she was flying, he could see that she was happy and he enjoyed the banter between Skyler and her crew.

At one point, they were headed to assist with the rescue of a skydiver from a cliff. The winds were choppy in the corridor between the vast cliffs, and the other chopper pilot had a smaller craft and wasn't able to get into the area to help evacuate the person. Sebastian had a headset on so he could hear all of the chatter between the crew and the two pilots.

"Rescue fourteen, this is Rescue seven," Skyler said into her mike.

"Go Rescue seven," came the reply.

"Come back fifteen, and clear," Skyler said.

"Back and clearing, roger that."

To Jams, Skyler said, "We're going to need to get in there close. What's my fuel?"

"Forty-five to bingo," Jams replied.

Skyler nodded. "Tom, Jerry, we're gonna need to make this quick. In and out, got it?"

"You got it boss!" Tom called, winking at Sebastian.

The first helicopter backed out of the way. As Skyler moved into position, the helicopter bucked.

"Sebo, you hold on back there," Skyler told him.

"Looking good, rescue seven," said the pilot of the other helicopter. "Come right ten,"

"Roger that, coming right ten. What do we got guys?" Skyler queried.

"I've got eyes on the target," Tom said. "Permission to open bay doors?"

"Roger that, open bay doors. Careful back there, this wind is a bitch."

"Roger that," Tom called as a blast of wind slammed into the copter.

"Son of a bitch!" Skyler yelled, as she fought the controls.

"Hurry up guys!" Jams called, glancing down at their instruments and then over at Skyler. "We may not be able to pull this one off."

"That kid's dead if we don't," Skyler countered, her look resolved.

Jams nodded, blowing his breath out, and redoubling his efforts to help Skyler control the aircraft.

Suddenly there was a loud noise and the helicopter shuddered.

"Fuck!" Skyler yelled. "Something hit the tail rotor!"

The helicopter started to spin slowly. Skyler fought the controls, there was a loud whine as Jams worked at restarting the rotor. It caught and the helicopter evened out again.

"Holy shit, Rescue seven!" yelled the other pilot over the comms. "Helluva recovery!"

"Thanks Rescue fourteen," Jams said, glancing over at Skyler.

Jams could see she was breathing heavily and looking shell shocked.

"Tom," Jams said, "I'm going to put us back in position, grab that kid and let's get home."

An hour later they were on the ground. Skyler hadn't said much on the way back. As soon as they powered down, she was out of the copter and striding down the flight line. Sebastian went to follow her, but Jams held him back.

"Give her a few," he told Sebastian.

Sebastian nodded, knowing that Jams knew his sister better than he did.

"Is she okay?" Sebastian asked Jams.

Jams looked hesitant, but nodded. "That was close," he said, his tone indicating how serious he was.

Sebastian nodded, swallowing nervously.

"But she did good," Sebastian said, remembering what the other pilot had said.

"She's a damned good pilot," Jams said, nodding. "Most people would have lost it there. And we'd have had to ditch."

"Ditch?" Sebastian asked.

"Drop the copter in the drink," Jerry said as he walked by, clapping Jams on the shoulder.

Sebastian's eyes widened, but he nodded, not trusting his voice at that moment, afraid it would shake if he tried to speak.

Three hours later, Devin came home. She'd gotten a text from Jams earlier that said, "Scary day at work, check on Sky."

Walking into the bedroom they shared, Devin could see Skyler sitting on the bed, her knees up to her chest, her arms draped over them. Devin could see the haunted look in her eyes immediately.

"Sky…" Devin began cautiously.

She saw Skyler's chin go up immediately.

Devin put her hands out in front of her in a defensive gesture. "Are you okay?" she asked, her voice soft as she walked over to the bed.

Skyler nodded, not looking at Devin, her eyes stared straight ahead.

Devin sat down on the bed, reaching out to touch Skyler's arm, her eyes searching Skyler for signs of injury.

"What happened?" she asked softly.

Skyler took a deep breath in, expelling is slowly, shaking her head. "Something hit our tail rotor," she said, her voice grave, "we almost lost her."

Devin nodded her head, her look apprehensive. She knew that this was likely to have put Skyler in the mind of the crash in Iraq, that's what was worrying her the most.

"But you're okay," Devin clarified.

"Yeah," Skyler said, her tone still haunted, "we recovered it."

"And everyone is okay?" Devin asked then.

Skyler looked over at her then, her eyes searching for hidden meaning behind Devin's questions. "Yeah," she said finally.

Devin nodded. "This scared you."

"It would scare anyone," Skyler said, her tone reproaching.

"Yes," Devin agreed, "but—"

"Don't," Skyler said.

"Skyler…" Devin began again.

"No!" Skyler practically yelled. "Just leave it," she said then, making a cutting gesture with her hand, her eyes flashing in anger.

Devin stood up, taking a step back, her look fearful.

Skyler looked back at her, challenging, her muscles tense, she was ready for a fight, and Devin could see that.

"This isn't going away, Skyler," Devin said.

Skyler just shook her head, her look annoyed.

"How long are we going to pretend?" Devin asked her then, her voice hinging on desperation.

"Pretend what?" Skyler snapped.

"That everything is okay, Skyler," Devin said, tears in her eyes suddenly, "that you're okay."

Skyler's head snapped back, like Devin had actually physically slapped her. Her eyes closed tiredly for a moment, then she shook her head.

"I'm not doing this right now," she said, her tone defeated and exhausted.

"Then when, Skyler?" Devin pleaded.

"Maybe never, Devin," Skyler said, her voice strident now. "Is that going to be a problem?"

Devin looked back at Skyler, surprised by Skyler's outright hostility suddenly. She could sense that things were coming to a head and she wasn't sure if she was ready for it, it scared her to death. Instead of answering, Devin just put her hands up in defeat, shaking her head. She walked out of the bedroom, closing the door softly. That night, Devin fell asleep on the couch. Skyler hadn't come out of the bedroom since the fight. Sebastian didn't know what was going on, but he didn't like the way things were. He knew there was serious tension, and he suspected it had to do with the near accident earlier that day.

Chapter 8

Things fell apart two days later.

Devin watched Skyler pacing back and forth in agitation in the backyard; she had no idea what to do, other than what she'd already done, which was to call Jams. Sebastian stood at the side of the sliding glass door, he had no idea what to do either. This wasn't the Skyler he knew and the idea that she was going off the rails scared him to death.

The conversation between Devin and Skyler that afternoon had started off simple enough; Devin was trying to get Skyler to go back to the doctors about the pain she was in. She'd been moving extremely gingerly since the near accident a few days before. Devin had gotten more of an explanation as to what had happened from Jams, and she suspected that Skyler was hurting more again due to the jarring motion of the helicopter spinning. She also knew that Skyler hadn't been sleeping at all over the last two days. Their CO had given them a few days off afterwards, knowing they needed time to deal with how close they'd come to crashing.

"You need more painkillers," Devin had said to Skyler, keeping her voice soft, easily sensing that this wasn't a topic Skyler was going to want to talk about.

"Leave it alone," Skyler had said, her tone even, but not angry.

"I'm worried about you babe," Devin had said, reaching out to touch Skyler's arm.

That's when Skyler's phone rang. She'd pulled the phone out of her pocket looking at the display. As Devin watched, all the blood drained out of Skyler's face. Without warning, Skyler had stood up and chucked her phone over the retaining wall in the backyard two hundred yards away. She swung her arm through and slammed it through the glass-top of the table. Devin had jumped up and out of the way of the shattering glass.

"Skyler!" Devin had yelled, seeing the scarlet color of blood on Skyler's hand. She'd tried to reach for Skyler's hand but Skyler yanked it away with a yell. She'd walked away from Devin then, and stood like a stone statue staring out over the ocean. She was cold and unapproachable. Devin had stood waiting for her to come back, but it didn't happen, she could see that Skyler's entire body was shaking, her hand, held down by her side, was dripping blood.

Devin had walked over and reached out to touch Skyler's shoulder, but Skyler had wrenched away from her. "Don't!" she'd yelled.

Devin had relented at that point, terrified beyond words, she knew she was watching Skyler fall apart, and it made her feel sick inside. Inside the house she'd encountered Sebastian, who'd been roused from his position on the couch when he'd heard the ruckus.

"What happened?" he'd asked, reaching for the sliding glass door handle.

Devin had shook her head. "Don't go out there, Sebastian," she'd told him. "I'm calling in back up."

She'd called Jams.

He arrived at the house forty-five minutes later.

"Where is she?" he asked.

Devin gestured to the backyard.

"Are you okay?" Jams asked her.

Devin nodded, tears in her eyes. "Please help her," she said, her voice shaking.

Jams walked over to her and hugged her. "I'll try," he told her, nodding to Sebastian who looked just as scared as Devin.

A minute later Jams was stepping out into the back yard. Skyler was at the edge of the yard, smoking and staring off into the distance. He noted that her body was completely rigid. When she dropped her hand holding the cigarette, he noticed the blood on her hand, and saw a small pool of blood below on the ground. He winced at the picture it presented.

"Hey," he said, finally.

Skyler glanced over her shoulder at him, narrowing her eyes, then turning her head back to look out over the ocean.

"She called you?" Skyler asked, her tone accusatory.

"She's terrified, Sky," he answered.

He didn't see her wince, but he wasn't completely surprised when she wheeled on him.

"So what the fuck are you gonna do?" she challenged.

Jams looked back at his partner of fifteen years, he could easily see the pain she was in, and he knew it wasn't just physical. He seriously doubted that she even felt the cuts to her hand.

"I'm going to try and talk ya down," Jams said, cautiously.

"Try leaving," Skyler said, turning around to light another cigarette.

"Yeah…" Jams said, "not gonna happen, pal."

Skyler shook her head, not looking back at him. She started pacing again, Jams leaned against one of the chairs, watching her, waiting her out.

It took a while, but he could see the fight start to leave her finally.

"Tell me what's goin' on, Sky," Jams said.

She shook her head again, taking a long drag on her cigarette, her face set in a determined line.

"The accident churned it up, didn't it?" Jams said, knowing his was right.

Skyler winced at the words, turning around again, her back to him.

"You don't have to answer," he said, "I know it." He took a couple of steps toward her, stopping when he saw her chin come up. "We need to get past this, Sky," he said then.

That had her wheeling on him again. "Really?!" she yelled. "You fucking think it's that easy?!"

He held his hands up in defensive gesture. "I didn't say it was going to be easy, Sky."

"You don't know," Skyler said, angry tears in her eyes.

"I know," Jams said, his tone sharp, "I was there, remember?"

"You were there," Skyler said, her tone snide. "You have no fucking idea!"

Jams pulled himself up short, wanting to rail right back at her, but knowing that it was what she wanted. She wanted to hit him, she wanted to hurt him, because she was in pain and she wanted to get it out of her. Throwing his arm up, he turned to stalk to the other side of the yard.

Devin watched from the window, feeling a sense of unreality. Sebastian stood mute, watching from behind Devin. She was praying that Jams knew what he was doing when he was dealing with Skyler. She saw that Skyler was pushing him, and it scared her to think of what would happen if either of them actually snapped and erupted in violence. She wondered if she'd been smart to call Jams; it was obvious they were both severely emotionally wounded by whatever had happened in Iraq, and maybe having them screaming at each other wasn't the smartest thing.

As she watched, Jams walked toward Skyler again, his posture more relaxed now.

"What happened today?" he asked Skyler, his voice quiet.

Skyler turned to look at him, she could see that he was trying to help her and part of her just wanted to crumble, but the fear that she'd never come back from it kept her from doing it.

Jams could see the devastation on her face and it hurt him to see it, but he stood steady, waiting for her to talk.

"Benny's mom called," Skyler said simply.

Jams sucked in his breath, knowing that would have been a big trigger for Skyler. Benny had been like her little brother; she'd loved the kid and missed him dearly.

"You should talk to her," Jams said, "she doesn't blame you."

Skyler gave a nasty snort of laughter. "Yeah, that's because she doesn't actually know what the fuck happened."

"She knows what happened," Jams said.

"Right, she knows the bullshit story the Army gave her," Skyler said, tears in her eyes, but her face contorted in anger.

Jams looked back at Skyler for a long time. "It wasn't your fault, Sky," he said finally.

"Don't fucking say that," Skyler growled.

Jams eyes flared at her tone. "It wasn't your fault, Skyler." His words measured as he gritted his teeth.

"Jams, don't fucking push me, man, I mean it," Skyler said then, her eyes blazing.

"It wasn't your fault, Skyler!"

"Shut up!" she screamed, throwing her lighter at him.

He ducked the lighter easily, and gave her a serious look. "It wasn't your fault," he said again.

Skyler gave a yell, and charged him, but he was ready for her. He grabbed her up in his arms, even as her forward motion shoved him back a few feet. He shoved her away from him, keeping his hands up to ward her off.

"Son of a fucking bitch!" she screamed, turning and stalking away from him.

"You need to deal with this Skyler, before you get us all killed," Jams said then, his tone low.

Skyler turned and looked at him, looking shaken by what he'd just said. "You're saying I'm unsafe now?" she asked, in disbelief.

"You're taking a lot of chances lately, and you know it," Jams countered.

Skyler nodded, her jaw twitching with the force of her clenching it so hard. "Then fucking call the CO, get me grounded, hell, fucking transfer!"

"Not gonna do that and you know it," Jams said.

"Why?" Skyler yelled.

"You know why," Jams said.

"Why, 'cause your fucking father told you it was your responsibility to watch out for me?" she practically spat in derision.

"Watch it," Jams said, his eyes narrowed. He knew she was lashing out, but there were some things that couldn't be taken back. "And no, that's not it, and you fucking know it."

"Then what is it?" Skyler asked, her tone sharp.

"You saved my life, you fucking idiot, and you know I'm not gonna let that go!"

"Try," Skyler retorted.

Jams shook his head, not believing how hardheaded this woman could be.

"Can't do it," Jams said, shaking his head.

"Then you're not trying hard enough," Skyler gritted out. "Just leave me the fuck alone, okay? Just leave!" Skyler yelled, shaking because she was ready to explode, everything was building and she just couldn't take anymore at this point.

"Skyler?" came Devin's voice from behind Jams.

Skyler visibly winced at Devin's tone, she sounded so scared. Skyler turned her back to them as she caught sight of Sebastian at the doorway to house. She didn't want to see the look of fear on Devin's face or the look of concern and fear that Sebastian wore.

She knew her world was crashing around her, and she knew she just couldn't take Devin's concern at that moment. Everything was spiraling out of control, and she had no idea how to stop it. Giving a loud yell, she slammed her hand into the rock wall in front of her, feeling bones in her hand break and realizing it felt good in some weird way.

Devin was beside her suddenly, reaching for her.

"Don't, Devin, God, please don't…" Skyler begging.

"Skyler, please…" Devin pleaded, as her fingers touched her arm.

Skyler closed her eyes, trying to ward off the weakening she could feel at the sound of Devin's voice and the feel of Devin's touch.

"Please…" Devin said again, sensing that Skyler was wavering.

Devin slid her arms around Skyler's waist from behind, resting her head against Skyler's back. Skyler felt the tears clogging her throat, and tried to force them back down. Devin's hands sliding up her stomach to her chest, to grip her shoulders from behind finally broke the tableau. Skyler bowed her head, letting the tears come not sure if she was ever going to be able to stop but unable to hold them back anymore.

Devin felt Skyler's body shaking and she knew she was crying, she just stayed where she was, her hands gripping Skyler's shoulders. After a few minutes Skyler seemed to have stopped.

Moving to stand in front of Skyler, Devin bent to look up into Skyler's eyes. "Please talk to me babe…" she said softly.

Skyler's blue-green eyes connected with hers, and Devin could see the naked pain in them.

"Tell her, Sky," Jams said. "Tell them." He gestured to Devin and Sebastian.

Slowly Skyler reached up into her pocket with her left hand, pulling out a cigarette and putting it on her mouth. Glancing over her shoulder, she grinned slightly at Jams.

"Think you could help a sista out?" Skyler asked.

Jams grinned, bending down to retrieve the lighter that Skyler had thrown at him and walked over to light the end of the cigarette obligingly for her.

"Oh Skyler…" Devin said, as she looked at Skyler's hand.

Skyler held her right hand up, looking at it as if it belonged to someone else. It was bruised and bleeding.

"Jesus, Skyler, there's glass…" Devin said, wincing.

Clenching her cigarette between teeth, Skyler lifted her right hand turning it so she could see the deep gash from when she broke the table glass. She noted absently the blood that was dripping down her arm as she held it up. Reaching over she gingerly pulled the piece of glass out of the cut, even as Devin gasped, "Skyler!"

Tossing the glass aside, Skyler moved to sit in a chair, feeling slightly light headed for a moment. Devin and Jams followed her cautiously, Sebastian walked up to stand near them.

Skyler sat smoking for a few minutes, trying to gather her thoughts. Jams took that time to step into the house and get a bottle of tequila, knowing if Skyler actually did start to talk, it was going to be rough. He also grabbed a towel for her hand.

Walking back outside, he handed Skyler the tequila. Skyler took a very long swig, feeling it burn down her throat. Taking the towel from Jams, she carefully wrapped it around her right hand. She was sitting with her legs spread, her arms on her knees, her head down. So Devin sat on the ground so she could look up at Skyler. Skyler held her cigarette in her left hand, picking at the threads on the towel absently as she started to talk.

"They shot out our tail rotor," she said, her voice even and toneless, her eyes were focused on a spot on the ground in front of her. "We went down hard," she said, her voice catching on the last word. "Radar was killed in the crash; the last thing I remembered was him yelling my name over and over..." her voice trailed off, as she swallowed against the tears that threatened to come again.

Devin winced at what she'd said, only able to imagine what that memory did to Skyler on a daily basis. Sebastian moved to sit in a chair, knowing he wasn't going to like what he was about to hear from his sister.

"We were all hurt," Skyler said, her eyes narrowing. "Benny was bad, but he was alive," She pressed her lips together for a moment. "We didn't even make it out of the copter,." She was bouncing her leg in agitation, her thoughts back in Iraq, at the scene of the crash. "They shot me, they shot Jams twice..." her voice trailed off.

"We were captured by insurgents," Jams put in, his look grave.

"Oh God..." Devin said, her voice a devastated whisper.

Skyler smiled a wintery smile, nodding her head. "Yeah, capturing American pilots was a big deal," she said, her voice sneering. "Better still, a *female* pilot..." she added, her voice trailing off as her throat constricted again. She remembered the voices, the knife held to her throat. She closed her eyes to try to force the memory out of her head.

Devin looked over at Jams and saw the devastation on his face, and she knew… she knew what the men had done and she was almost sure she was going to be sick.

"Skyler…" she breathed.

Skyler forced her tears back, only to choke on them a moment later. "Benny died trying to stop them."

"No…" Devin said, crying now. "Oh Skyler…" she said, unable to think of anything to say that would help at that moment.

Tears were streaming down Skyler's cheeks at this point.

"What happened?" Devin asked. "How did you get away?"

"We escaped," Skyler said simply.

Devin looked at Jams, and she could see that he was waiting for Skyler to say more.

When she didn't, he canted his head to the side. "What she's not telling you is that she took them all out, every one of them. She saved my life," he said, his eyes on his partner.

"That's why you got the Medal of Honor," Devin said, looking up at Skyler who simply nodded her head.

Sebastian sat quietly listening to the story and feeling the reality of it kick in. He felt a sense of helplessness and could only imagine how Skyler felt.

"Those nightmares you've been having," Devin said, her tone cautious still. "Those were about that time, weren't they?"

Skyler nodded, looking guilty. She'd always told Devin that she didn't remember what they were about.

Devin nodded, accepting that. "And when that guy in Las Vegas put his hands on you…"

"I snapped," Skyler said, "can't handle men grabbing at me like that."

Devin nodded. "That makes sense."

"So this morning…" Devin began, wanting to know what had set Skyler off.

"Benny's mom called," Skyler said.

Devin nodded, waiting for the rest of the explanation.

"Benny was the little brother that I'd left behind," Skyler said, looking over at Sebastian sadly. "He was so much like you," she told Sebastian, her eyes haunted. "The idea that he died trying to protect me…" She shook her head as her voice trailed off.

"His mother doesn't know that," Jams said. "The Army cleansed the official story to remove any indication of what happened to Sky, or any of us while we were in their hands." He looked over at Sky, knowing it was part of what ate at her constantly. "Benny's mom thinks he died as a result of his injuries in the crash."

Devin looked at Skyler again. "Is that what you want her to think?"

Skyler looked back at her for a long moment, then shrugged. "Never really thought about it."

"You just think it's your fault," Jams said quietly.

"It is," Skyler said simply.

"Yeah," Jams said, narrowing his eyes at her, "it is *your* fault that Benny loved you so much that he was willing to die to try to protect you. You took care of that kid, from day one. Every time he did something stupid, you fixed it for him, every time he got caught with his cell phone you took the heat. If he showed up late for duty, you covered for him. You talked him down when his girlfriend broke up with him, you helped him bag that Army nurse… he loved you, Sky, that's why he died for you."

Skyler was crying by the time he finished.

"Maybe I should have treated him like a commanding officer would, then he might be alive," Skyler said.

"No," Jams said, "he would have died from his injuries Sky, you know that. This way he died trying to protect you."

"He died a hero," Devin put in, tears on her cheeks as well.

"Yeah," Sebastian put in, "he died trying to save my sister, he was a hero."

Skyler looked between the two of them, seeing the certainty on their faces.

"Maybe that's what you need to tell Benny's mom," Jams said, "that he died a hero."

Skyler looked at him, and he could see that she was considering the idea.

"We've got the reunion coming up," Jams said. "You know they keep asking if you'll be there this time."

"Reunion?" Devin asked.

"Of our unit," Jams replied. Benny and Radar's parents always attend, and they're always looking for Sky, but she doesn't come. She can't deal with them."

"Maybe we should go," Devin said, her look taking in Sebastian.

Reaching out, Devin touched Skyler's knee. "Sky?"

Skyler looked at her, her eyes still so sad. After a long moment, she nodded slowly. Devin leaned up, kissing Skyler's lips softly.

"Now can we take you to the doctor to have them look at your hand?" Devin asked.

Skyler chuckled nodding her head.

Three hours after arriving for their Emergency Room visit, they found that Skyler had broken a couple of bones in her hand and needed six stitches in the same hand to close the wound made by the glass. Fortunately, there'd been no major nerve damage. By the time Jams drove them all back to the house in Malibu, Skyler was asleep on the backseat with her head in Devin's lap.

The guys helped Skyler into the house, Devin got her ready for bed and essentially tucked her in, kissing her lips softly.

"I'll be right outside," she told Skyler, "and I'll come to bed soon, okay?"

Skyler nodded tiredly, already half asleep again. The painkillers they'd given her at the hospital, as well as the events of the day, were taking effect.

Devin walked back out to the living room, seeing Jams and Sebastian sitting on the couch.

"So…" she said, feeling the impact of everything she'd learned that day.

"Yeah…" Jams said, his tone worn out.

Devin sat down, shaking her head. "It's a wonder she didn't explode before now," she said.

Jams chuckled. "I don't think you understand."

"What do you mean?" Devin asked.

"Without you," Jams said, "I don't know that she would have ever dealt with any of this."

"How could she function with all of that in her head?" Devin asked.

"She blocked it out," Jams said, "she was ice cold, Devin, and then you came along."

"She's been one tough cookie," Devin said, grinning.

"Yeah, but you have no idea how much different she's been since she's been seeing you," he told her.

"That different?" she asked, unable to believe what he was saying.

"Oh yeah," Jams said, "trust me on that."

"She was never like that before," Sebastian put in. "When we were kids, she was always so much fun. Even with the way dad was, she just shrugged it off."

"She learned to block things out early on," Jams told him.

Sebastian looked surprised by what Jams said, but then nodded. "Yeah, I guess you're right." He looked at Devin then. "I guess she's lucky to have you," he said, smiling, then looked over at Jams, "and you."

Jams shook his head. "If it wasn't for her I wouldn't be here," he said, "so it's me that owes her."

"How'd she do it?" Sebastian asked. "How'd she take them out?"

Jams looked back at Sebastian, grimacing. "It was pretty bloody," he told him, "trust me, you don't want details. Suffice it to say that she was brutal, and she definitely made them sorry they ever messed with her."

Later that night, Devin walked into the bedroom, seeing that Skyler was still asleep. She was happy to see that, she knew Skyler hadn't been sleeping well lately. Walking over to the bed, she looked at Skyler's bandaged hand, it looked okay, no blood was visible, which had been what the doctor had told her to watch for.

Devin went in and took a shower, then walked back in the bedroom. She saw that Skyler's eyes were open.

"I'm sorry," Devin said, "did I wake you?"

Skyler shook her head. "No," she said simply.

Skyler held her left hand out to Devin, who took it, moving to lie down next to Skyler.

"How do you feel?" Devin asked, noting that Skyler still looked tired.

"Like I'm swimming underwater in a rain coat," Skyler said. "I hate pain meds."

"I know, babe," Devin said, "but you need the rest and being out of pain for a little while is probably not a bad thing."

Skyler nodded, her look searching as she did.

"Look," Skyler began, her voice soft, "I'm really sorry about today."

"It's okay, Skyler," Devin said, her voice quiet too.

"No," Skyler said, shaking her head, "you were scared, and I scared you, and that's not okay."

"I wasn't afraid of you, Sky, I was afraid *for* you," Devin said, her eyes searching Skyler's.

"What were you afraid of?" Skyler asked.

"I was afraid you weren't going to let any of us help you," Devin told her.

Skyler closed her eyes, her look pained. "I'm sorry about that too."

"There's nothing to be sorry about, Sky," Devin said, putting her hand to Skyler's cheek. "With what you've been through, anyone else would have lost it a long time ago. What's important here is that you let us help you now."

Skyler looked unhappy with that. "Dev…" she began, shaking her head as her voice trailed off, "this is so much, and why should you have to deal with it?"

"Because I love you, Skyler," Devin said, "because I want to help you through this, I want to give you anything you need to help you."

"Why?" Skyler asked her look disbelieving.

"Let me ask you something," Devin said. "When I was trapped in my car, and I called you, why did you come?"

Skyler looked back at Devin as if she'd just lost her mind. "I had to," Skyler said, though it was obvious Devin actually wanted a real answer.

"But why?" Devin asked.

"Because…" Skyler began, but stopped, as she shook her head again.

"Because you love me," Devin said, tears in her eyes now. "And I have to come for you Skyler," she said, her tone intense, "I have to find you, and I have to save you, because I love you."

"Save me, huh?" Skyler asked her look tender.

Devin nodded, tears streaming down her cheeks now. Skyler reached up to brush Devin's tears away. Leaning down, Skyler kissed Devin's lips softly, wanting more than anything to erase the sad look in Devin's eyes and knowing there was only one way. She was going to have to do the work.

"So," Skyler said, "how do we do that?"

Devin smiled. "I think we need to find someone for you to talk to," she said cautiously, considering the reactions Skyler had to that kind of statement previously.

Skyler detected the wariness in Devin's voice and grimaced at it. "I guess I haven't been exactly open to that idea before, have I?"

"Not exactly," Devin said.

Skyler nodded, expelling her breath slowly. "Okay," she said so simply that Devin was shocked.

"Oh… okay," Devin said, having been prepared to explain to Skyler at length why talking to someone would be good for her, and so on. Not having to do that threw her off a bit.

Skyler chuckled at her flustered look. "Expected a bigger fight on that, huh?"

"Kinda," Devin said, her tone joking.

Skyler pinned her with a look. "I want to do whatever it takes to deal with this," she said, "and I know it's not going to be quick or easy."

"Good," Devin said, nodding.

Devin could see that Skyler was getting heavy lidded again, so she lay with her head in the hollow of Skyler's shoulder, her hand stroking Skyler's waist until she heard Skyler's breathing become even.

By the time Skyler got up the next morning, Devin had looked up a number of therapists in the area and was ready to tell Skyler about them.

Skyler walked into the kitchen, bleary eyed. Devin was sitting at the kitchen table, she got up, kissed Skyler on the lips and guiding her to a chair. She then got her coffee handing it to her.

"Do you want anything for breakfast?" Devin asked, knowing that Skyler was likely to be hungry since she hadn't eaten the night before.

Skyler shook her head. "Too tired, can't think."

Devin grinned, turning back to the kitchen and made Skyler some toast, figuring that wasn't too difficult to deal with. Skyler raised an eyebrow at the plate when Devin put it in front of her, but picked up a corner of toast anyway, eating it quietly.

"So," Devin said, sitting down next to Skyler, "I've taken the liberty of looking up some local therapists…" She let her voice trail off as she looked for Skyler's reactions.

Skyler merely nodded, continuing to eat the toast. She reminded Devin of a small child, focusing on one thing at a time. It made her smile fondly.

"What?" Skyler asked, catching the smile.

"You're just very cute, right now," Devin said, grinning.

"Cute?" Skyler repeated her look doubtful.

"Cute," Devin said again, "get over it." The last was said with a wink.

Skyler grinned. "So therapists," she said, the word sounding really foreign to her.

"Yes," Devin said, grabbing her iPad and pulling it over to her, "I found a Dr. Sandra Dobson, she has a lot of experience with PTSD, and she's formerly military, Army in fact."

"PTSD?" Skyler repeated her look skeptical.

"I think clinically what you have would be called Post Traumatic Stress Disorder, babe," Devin said, knowing that it was the stigma of the term that was bothering Skyler.

Skyler gave a grimace of distaste, but nodded all the same.

"There are others," Devin said, scrolling through the list of names and qualifications, "but I think that this Dr. Dobson seems like she'd be the most relatable."

Skyler nodded, blowing her breath out in a sigh.

"She has an opening today…" Devin said, her tone hopeful.

Skyler gave her a pointed look that said "Really?" but she simply said, "Fine."

Three hours later Devin and Skyler were sitting in the outer office of Dr. Sandra Dobson. Devin had been surprised when Skyler had asked her to come with her. She was more surprised when the doctor opened the door to invite Skyler in, and Skyler held Devin's hand, pulling her gently up with her.

"You want me to come in?" Devin asked Skyler.

Skyler looked back at her for a long moment. "This is where you'll find me," she said, a wistful smile on her lips.

Devin nodded, and followed Skyler into the doctor's office.

The office was light and airy, furnished with comfortable chairs.

Skyler raised an eyebrow. "No couch?" she asked the doctor.

"I'm not that kind of doctor," the doctor replied with a wink, then she extended her hand to Skyler. "I'm Sandra, you can call me Sandy."

Skyler took her hand, shaking it. "Skyler," she said.

"Nice to meet you Skyler," Sandy said, smiling, then she looked to Devin.

"I'm Devin," Devin said, nodding.

"Nice to meet you Devin."

When the three of them were seated, Sandy looked between the two of them.

"So what brings you in?"

Skyler was looking around the room, seeing pictures on the wall, even spotting a picture of a team in front of an Army helicopter. She then focused her attention back on the doctor.

"Everyone's worried about me," Skyler told her.

Sandy looked back at her. "Do they have good reason to be?" she asked simply.

Skyler considered the question. "I think I've given them reason to, yeah."

Sandy nodded, then pinned Skyler with a look. "Are you worried about yourself?"

Skyler looked back at that other woman, her lips twitched as she thought about her answer.

Finally, she nodded. "Sometimes," she answered honestly.

"Hooah," Sandy said quietly.

Next to Skyler, Devin smiled, thinking that this was definitely the right place.

An hour later, Skyler had answered questions, and they'd talked generally about the crash, but hadn't gotten too deep at that point.

"We'll get our boots muddy next time," Sandy said, with a wink when they left.

Skyler and Devin had lunch at a nearby restaurant. After they'd ordered, Devin looked over at Skyler, her look assessing.

"What?" Skyler asked, sensing that Devin wanted to ask something, but was hesitant.

"Are you okay?" Devin asked. "I mean, was that okay?"

Skyler grinned, nodding. "It was fine," she said, wanting to put Devin at ease.

"Do you think you're going to be able to talk to her?" Devin asked.

Skyler considered the question, then nodded. "Yeah, she seems okay."

"Okay, good."

A week later, Skyler had been to see Sandy three times. Devin hadn't gone with her for those appointments, wanting to give Skyler the space to be open with Sandy. One night after a session, Devin woke to feel Skyler moving restlessly, her hand at Devin's waist was grasping and loosening over and over.

"Sky," Devin said softly, touching her shoulder.

Skyler's eyes flew open, and she looked around her breathing heavily.

"It's okay," Devin said softly.

Skyler looked down at her, nodding slowly.

"Nightmare?" Devin asked.

"Yeah," Skyler said, reaching up to rub her eyes, as if to rub the image out of her head.

"Bad one?" Devin asked then.

Skyler looked back at her for a long moment, wanting to dismiss the dream like she usually did. She hesitated then she blew her breath out.

"Not as bad as some," she said, relaxing against the pillows again.

"The crash?" Devin asked.

"Yeah," Skyler said, "but in this one Benny was okay, and was telling me it would be okay…" her voice trailed off sadly.

Devin, moved to sit up, looking down at Skyler.

"What was he like?" Devin asked, hoping that she wouldn't upset Skyler by asking.

Skyler smiled, looking sad at the same time. "He was a kid," she said, her tone reflecting her sadness. "But he was smart, and he knew how to make everyone laugh. Whenever I'd try to be the tough commander with him, he'd pull the face…"

"The face?" Devin asked.

"Yeah, the pouty little boy face, and I'd feel like shit, worked every friggin' time too," she said, her smile indicating that it didn't really bother her that much that Benny had that kind of power. "He actually asked to be assigned to me. He said that he knew he could learn stuff from me… I never figured out what stuff he wanted to learn, he just moved into the group and became a part of us."

"He was smart, he knew who to align himself with," Devin said, winking at Skyler.

Skyler gave a brief laugh. "He was worse than a puppy with his big blue eyes… he got away with a lot with me."

Devin smiled fondly, she could see that Skyler had truly cared about the young man.

"Where was he from?" Devin asked.

"Texas. "That was his other big thing, trying to get us all to go to Texas to his parents' ranch." Her eyes misted over at that point.

Devin moved to hug Skyler gently.

Pulling back, she looked down at Skyler again. "Maybe the dream was his way of communicating with you now," Devin told her.

Skyler looked back at her for a long minute, surprised by the statement, but then she nodded, part of her wanting that to be the case.

They went back to sleep not too long after that. Devin was relieved that Skyler was finally sharing some of her pain. It felt better than to have Skyler claim she was fine, when Devin knew that wasn't true.

The next morning, Skyler slept in, while Devin got up. Devin was sitting in the kitchen drinking coffee when Sebastian came into the kitchen. Devin smiled up at him. Sebastian returned the smile, and reached for a cup for coffee. He sat down at the table with his coffee, and looked over at Devin.

"How's she doing?" Sebastian asked, it was something he'd been wanting to check in on.

He'd started the academy a few days before, so he hadn't been home before Skyler and Devin were asleep the last few nights.

Devin nodded. "She's doing good," she said honestly. "She's still having nightmares, but they aren't as bad or as often."

Sebastian nodded, then shook his head. "I really can't get over all that she's gone through."

"It's a lot," Devin said, "that's for sure."

"I'm really glad she has you," Sebastian said then, his look earnest. "I'm not sure anyone else would have gotten her to do what you have. Jams told me how hard and closed off she was until she met you. He said, she's changed a lot since she's been dating you."

Devin smiled softly. "She's definitely gotten more open with me, but until that huge thing…" she said, gesturing to the back yard to indicate what had occurred back there. "I really couldn't get her to talk about the crash."

"Well, she's doing it now," Sebastian said, "and that's a good thing."

"It is," Devin agreed.

"Has she talked anymore about going to that reunion thing?" Sebastian asked.

"No," Devin said, shaking her head, "I'm not even sure when it is exactly."

"Jams said it's next month," Sebastian said. "He said it's in Texas this year."

"She might get to that ranch after all," she murmured.

"Huh?" Sebastian queried.

"Nothing," Devin said, smiling.

Later that morning, Skyler and Devin were walking along the beach, something they hadn't previously done, but had started doing when Skyler went into therapy. It seemed to help Skyler process things.

"Sebastian asked me something this morning," Devin said, watching as Skyler threw a rock into the oncoming waves.

"What?" Skyler asked, glancing back at Devin.

"He asked if you'd said anymore about going to that unit reunion," Devin told her.

Skyler turned to look at her. "He did?"

"Yeah," Devin said, "Jams told him it was next month."

Skyler nodded.

"In Texas," Devin added.

It was clear from Skyler's look that she hadn't known that part of it. She turned back to the ocean and stared out over it for a long time. Devin walked up behind her, sliding her hands around Skyler's waist, and putting her head against Skyler's back. She felt Skyler's hands cover hers. They stood that way for a long time. Then Skyler turned around to look at her.

"I guess I'm going to the ranch," she said with a grin.

"I was hoping you'd say that," Devin replied, smiling.

Chapter 9

The reunion was being held in San Antonio, Texas, in a restaurant along the famed River Walk along the San Antonio River. The restaurant, called the Iron Cactus, had a banquet room that the reunion was being held in.

"Voodoo, you made it…" said Acorn, his booming voice announcing to everyone that Skyler was there.

Almost as one the crowd turned to look at the small group that had just entered.

Skyler was dressed in all black; the look she wore reflected the somber attire. The rest of their group was dressed more casually. Devin looked at the other attendees, she could see varying degrees of pain or sadness, which was quickly replaced with smiles and call outs to Skyler and Jams.

Skyler headed straight for the bar, located at the back of the room they were in. She ordered a double shot of tequila, knocking it back immediately. Devin stood by, looking around, but keeping her eye on Skyler.

Jams, Devin and Sebastian had talked before the trip, agreeing that if they thought things were getting too tough for Skyler, they'd get her out of the place. Devin had actually spoken to Sandy about the trip, asking if she felt Skyler could handle the situation. Sandy had said that she thought it might be good for Skyler to finally face those demons but that they shouldn't let things overwhelm her. Devin intended to make sure that didn't happen.

After a few minutes, the foursome made their way to a table. Devin ordered food for them, wanting to make sure Skyler ate something, since she was now drinking a beer.

Not too long after the food arrived, an older couple walked over to the table. Devin saw Jams hand reach over to touch Skyler on the shoulder. Skyler, who had been talking to Sebastian, turned to look at Jams, and followed the direction of his look. Both Skyler and Jams moved to stand from the table, the look on their faces serious.

"Mr. and Mrs. O'Reilly," Jams said, extending his hand to the man first.

Devin felt herself holding her breath as she glanced over at Sebastian, who looked equally nervous.

The couple shook hands with Jams, and then looked to Skyler who was standing at what Devin could only consider attention.

"Sir," Skyler said, inclining her head to the man. "Ma'am," she said to the woman then, her look conciliatory.

"We're so happy to see you here," the woman said, then she turned to look at Devin and Sebastian.

"Ma'am," Skyler said, gesturing to Devin, "this is Devin James, my girlfriend." she smiled at Devin.

Devin stood, extending her hand to the woman.

"I'm Anna," the woman said, smiling at Devin. "This is John," she said, gesturing to her husband. "We're Tommy's parents."

Devin nodded, glancing at Skyler.

"Radar's parents," Skyler told her.

"I thought so," Devin said, smiling at the woman.

"And this is my brother Sebastian," Skyler said, introducing her brother as he moved to stand.

"Good to meet you," Anna said, shaking Sebastian's hand.

"You too, ma'am," Sebastian replied, nodding to John respectfully.

"Let's sit," Anna said, as John grabbed two chairs from nearby tables.

Once they were all seated, Anna turned to Skyler, taking her hands in her own. "I want you to know that my son loved being on your team," she told Skyler.

Skyler closed her eyes for a moment, nodding, even as her throat constricted. Devin reached out, putting her hand to Skyler's back. A tear fell from Skyler's eyes.

"He said you were the best damned pilot in the unit," John told Skyler.

"Thank you sir," Skyler said, looking at him, her eyes glazed with tears. "Your son did a great job as a crew member."

"We miss him," Jams added.

Skyler nodded, agreeing with Jams. Not trusting herself to speak.

"We also understand," John said, his tone subdued, "that if it wasn't for you, we wouldn't have gotten his body back so we could lay him to rest."

Skyler turned her head away, as the memory ran through her mind. It had been a tough job, getting Radar out. He'd been a fairly good sized guy and at that point she could barely breathe due to a punctured lung and broken ribs, not to mention the gunshot wound. But she'd had no intention of leaving any of her men behind.

"Leave no man behind," Jams said, knowing what she'd been thinking.

He held up his beer to Skyler. Skyler looked over at him and picked up her beer. "Angels Fall," she said, and with that they clinked the ends of the bottles together as the group looked on.

"Chief," came a voice from behind them.

Skyler recognized it immediately.

"Gunny," she said, moving to stand, and was immediately caught up in a bear hug.

The man was introduced as Gunnery Sergeant Smitty. As they talked, Radar's parents stood from the table and looked on. At one point, Anna walked over to Skyler, moving to hug her. Skyler hugged the woman back, feeling the extra squeeze Anna gave her. She appreciated that Anna seemed to understand how hard it was for her to talk about the crash. John extended his hand to Skyler, taking it and shaking it firmly. The couple then walked away, circulating amongst the group.

Not too long after that there was a toast to the fallen soldiers. Radar and Benny were then remembered specifically, fortunately they'd been the only soldiers lost from the unit. After the toast, Skyler did some circulating and came face to face with Benny's parents. Jams saw it from across the room and grabbed Devin by the hand taking her with him to intercept the group.

"We finally get to meet you," Benny's mother was saying. "I'm Jessie," she said, smiling at Jams as he walked up.

Jessie Kings looked just like her son, her blue eyes shining as she looked up at Skyler.

"This is Billy's dad, Bill Senior," Jessie said, pulling her husband forward.

Billy's dad was a big man, with the chiseled features of a John Wayne type cowboy. He nodded to Skyler, a man of few words.

Skyler nodded to Bill Senior, her look pained. She felt Devin's hand take hers. Glancing at Devin, she could see that Devin was watching her. Jams stood nearby doing the same. She squeezed Devin's hand smiling at her. She caught sight of Sebastian then, he stood close to Jams. The whole gang was there, Skyler thought to herself.

"Mrs. Kings," Skyler said, "this is Devin, my girlfriend, and that's Sebastian, my brother."

"It's good to meet all of you," Jessie said, nodding, then she looked back at Skyler. "We were hoping that you'd be willing to come back to the ranch with us," she said, her tone entreating.

Skyler nodded. "We'd like that. I have some things I'd like to tell you."

"Well, we can do that there," Jessie said, smiling softly.

By the time the reunion wound down, it was nearly midnight. Jessie suggested that Skyler and the group follow them to the ranch.

"It's about a half hour out of town," she told them.

Since Skyler had had a few drinks, Jams took over driving. Devin and Skyler were in the backseat. Devin looked over at Skyler.

"Are you okay?" she asked.

Skyler nodded, taking Devin's hand in hers. It was at that moment that the song "Angels Fall" came on in the car, Skyler's iPod was plugged into the stereo.

"Fuckin' Benny!" Jams said, grinning, even as he turned the song up.

The group listened to the song, Skyler sang the words.

Devin wondered if Skyler meant to let things go finally. She hoped that's what she'd meant. After the song ended, Skyler looked over at Devin, seeing the concern in Devin's eyes.

Leaning in, she kissed Devin's lips, pulling back to look down into her eyes.

"I couldn't have done this without you," she told Devin.

Devin smiled back at her. "I think you could have."

"Uh-uh." Skyler shook her head. "Jams, hand me my iPod," she said, tapping the back of the driver's seat.

Jams handed her the iPod. Skyler took it, scrolling through the songs, selecting one, then looking at Devin.

"You need to listen to this," Skyler told Devin. "Especially the first verse."

Devin nodded, and listened as the song began, she could see the name of the song was, "You're Mine" by Disturbed.

The first verse told Devin everything she needed to know. It talked about how Skyler's life of misery was beating her down, and that she'd gotten her strength back and it was all because Devin belonged to her.

As the song played on, Devin looked back at Skyler in wonder. "Is that how you really feel?"

"Definitely," Skyler replied, unwavering.

Devin smiled, leaning in to kiss Skyler deeply. They hugged, and stayed that way for a while.

In the front seat, Sebastian and Jams exchanged looks, Jams nodded by way of telling Sebastian that what they'd just heard was a really good thing. Now if they could just get through this visit with Benny's parents...

The ranch they drove up to was expansive, much larger than Jams or Skyler had expected. This was a serious cattle ranch and Billy had never let on that he was from such a successful family. Skyler and Jams exchanged a look as they climbed out of the car, Jams look was glowering, even as Skyler shrugged, grinning.

Benny's parents lead them into the huge white house that seemed to go on and on. The foyer they walked into was two stories and decorated with rich wood and rustic style paintings and bronze Remington statues.

"Wow..." Sebastian said, staring above him.

Jessie and Bill Senior grinned.

"It's late," Jessie said, tiredly, "so we're gonna just show you to your rooms, and we'll talk in the morning, okay?"

Skyler nodded, grateful for the short reprieve.

Within the hour, Devin and Skyler were lying in the massive bed in one of the guest rooms. The room was large, with its own bathroom and a bare timber ceiling.

"I take it you weren't expecting anything like this," Devin said, leaning up to look at Skyler.

"Got that right," Skyler said, shaking her head. "Benny never said that the ranch he was from was this massive."

Devin grinned. "Maybe he wanted to be just a regular guy."

"Yeah," Skyler said, nodding, "makes sense. He was always trying to fit in; I guess we didn't know why it was so important to him."

They were both silent for a few minutes, each lost in their own thoughts. Devin looked up at Skyler then, seeing that she was deep in thought.

"How are you feeling about this?" Devin asked, feeling like she needed to check in on Skyler's state of mind.

Skyler looked down at her. "I'm scared as hell," she told her honestly.

Devin grimaced, nodding her head. "You have to know that it'll be okay," she said.

Skyler inhaled slowly, her look skeptical. "Do I?"

"What's the worst thing that could happen?" Devin asked. "What are you imagining?"

Skyler thought about the question. "I guess I'm worried about what they'll say."

"What are you planning to tell them?" Devin asked.

"Everything," Skyler replied simply.

Devin inhaled sharply, but then nodded slowly.

"You're worried that they'll blame you."

Skyler looked back at her for a long moment, then nodded.

"It wasn't your fault," Devin said, knowing that this was something that Sandy had been working on with Skyler for the last month.

"I know," Skyler said too quickly, nodding her head.

"Skyler…" Devin said, her tone chiding, "you know it wasn't your fault, none of that was your fault."

Skyler grimaced, her guilt warring with her common sense.

Devin levered herself up on her elbow, her hand reaching out to touch Skyler's cheek.

"No matter what happens," Devin told her, "we will get through this."

Skyler looked back at her, swallowing convulsively, even as she nodded.

They fell asleep that night, with Devin's hand on Skyler's chest, Skyler's hand covering Devin's.

Skyler woke in the middle of the night with the sensation that she was being watched. Looking across the room she was shocked to see Benny standing there.

"What are you doing here?" she asked him.

"Saying goodbye," Benny said, his blue eyes sparkling in the semi-darkness.

"Don't do that."

"Gotta."

"No," Skyler said, shaking her head in futility.

"Ya gotta let me go…" Billy said as he faded from sight.

Skyler woke with a start, looking around she didn't see anything out of place. She realized then that she'd been dreaming. Laying back, she hugged Devin close, trying to shake off the feeling of the dream.

The next morning dawned and Devin woke before Skyler. She got out of bed carefully, and pulled on jeans and a t-shirt, tiptoeing out of the bedroom, hoping she could find Jams. She ran into him in the hallway.

"Hey," Jams said, grinning because he was sure they'd been doing the same thing: trying to locate each other to talk before Skyler got up.

"Hi," Devin said, returning his grin.

"How's she doing?" Jams asked without preamble.

"She's okay, she's scared though."

"What is she going to tell them?"

"Everything, she said," Devin told him.

"Wow," Jams said, looking surprised, but then he nodded. "It might be what she needs to do, to get past all of this."

"I'm just hoping that they take it okay," she said, voicing her biggest concern.

There was no way to know how Jessie and Bill were going to take what Skyler would tell them about their son and the true circumstances of his death. Jams and Devin, however, were resolved to back Skyler up, no matter what happened.

Jams and Devin were sitting out on the large patio, when Sebastian joined them. The patio was furnished with chairs and couches, set on large terracotta tiles with Spanish tile inserts. There was a built in fireplace, a barbeque set off to the side, and a huge blue pool nearby. The morning was cool with the slightest breeze, it was a beautiful morning.

"How's she doing?" Sebastian asked immediately.

"She's okay," Devin told him, nodding and smiling at him. "A bit nervous, but for the most part, okay."

"Good," Sebastian said, looking relieved then looked around him. "This place is insane!"

Devin and Jams chuckled.

"Is this what you were expecting?" Sebastian asked then, suspecting that it wasn't.

"Nope. Benny never told us any of this," he said, gesturing to the expansive patio they sat on, indicating the huge house as well. "He said he was from a ranch in Texas."

"That was our Billy," Jessie said from behind them.

She'd seen them out on the patio and had stepped outside to tell them that there was coffee and breakfast in the dining room. She'd overheard the comments, including the ones about Skyler.

The group got up from their chairs, turning to look at Jessie.

"He never wanted people to know he came from all this," Jessie said, smiling fondly. "He wanted to be a regular guy." Her look turned sad then. "I guess that's why he joined the Army."

"To be a regular guy?" Jams asked, his tone gentle.

Jessie nodded. "And to be anonymous."

"You should know that Skyler adored your son," Jams told Jessie.

"And he adored her," Jessie said, smiling as tears glazed her eyes in the morning sunlight. "When he first wrote to us about joining your team, and told us about Skyler, we actually thought she was someone he was interested in romantically."

Jams grinned, he'd long suspected that Benny had a crush on Skyler. Skyler had never been flagrant about her sexuality, but she also didn't hide it. It had taken some time for Benny to realize that Skyler wasn't really interested in guys.

"I do think he had a case of puppy love for her," Jams told Jessie honestly. "Sky wasn't shy about who she was, but she also didn't shake your hand with one hand and pull out her lesbian card with the other."

Jessie chuckled at that description. "He did eventually tell us that Skyler was gay, but that she was still really cool and that we'd like her a lot."

It was Jams turn to chuckle, the words Jessie had used sounded exactly like Benny.

"We also thought his nickname was cute," Jessie said.

Jams dropped his head. "He drove us crazy with that band!"

Jessie laughed. "Us too!" Then she stepped back, gesturing to the house. "I wanted to let you all know that there's coffee and breakfast in the dining room if you're interested?"

"Definitely," Sebastian said, walking toward the house, the rest of the group followed.

Devin lagged behind to talk to Jessie. "Skyler's not up, yet. I don't think she slept very well, the night before last."

Jessie nodded, understanding.

"Well, we'll just let her sleep then," she said, patting Devin on the arm with a smile.

When they all had coffee and plates of food in front of them, Jessie looked over at Devin.

"How long have you two been together?" she asked.

"About a year now," Devin said.

"She still seems kind of haunted," Jessie said, with concern.

"She took the loss of her crew very hard," Devin told her, looking over at Jams.

"She's just now starting to really deal with it," Jams told Jessie.

Jessie nodded, sensing that they were trying to protect Skyler, and prepare her at the same time. Her son's death had been the hardest thing Jessie Kings had ever been through. She'd seen Skyler and Jams at the air field when her son's body had come home; they'd been two of the pall bearer's escorting his coffin off the plane, and again at the funeral. Jessie had been far too mired in her own pain then to pay any attention to the two members of Billy's crew that had survived. Later she'd tried to send a letter to them, but never heard back. She'd left it alone after that.

When she'd met Jams at the first reunion, she'd still been unable to really talk about Billy's death, so they'd exchanged pleasantries and talked about minor things. This was the first time Jessie had actually talked about Billy's death with the members of his crew that had survived. She was as nervous as it sounded like Skyler was about this meeting.

Bill Senior walked into the dining room, poured himself a cup of coffee and, picking up a roll, he joined them at the table. Nodding to everyone, he sat quietly and drank his coffee.

"So," Jessie said, looking at Jams. "What are you doing now?"

"Sky and I work for Los Angeles Fire Department's Air Operations," Jams told her.

"They rescue people," Sebastian put in, he'd been silent most of the morning, but he wanted to make sure that Benny's parents understood that his sister saved people's lives now.

Jessie and Bill Senior exchanged a look, knowing exactly why Sebastian made that statement. They'd had a number of discussions about wanting to talk to Skyler Boché and Daniel Laurent. Bill Senior wanted to leave things alone, but knew that it was eating his wife up inside, and didn't want her to suffer. He was also afraid of what he'd hear about his son if he let them tell them.

Jessie nodded at Jams, smiling. "It sounds like its right up your alley."

"Skyler does the piloting, but I help," Jams said, grinning.

"And you know the difference between a copilot and a duck, right?" Skyler asked from the doorway of the dining room.

"Ducks can actually fly," Jams answered, giving his partner a narrowed look and a wide grin.

That had everyone chuckling. Skyler walked over, leaning down to kiss Devin. She looked around at everyone then.

"Good morning," she said to the group as she sat down in the chair next to Devin's.

Good mornings were murmured, as Devin got up to fix Skyler some coffee. Skyler watched Devin getting her coffee, smiling fondly as she recognized that Devin was trying to smooth things over for her.

Devin turned back to the table, handing Skyler her coffee with a wink.

"Thanks," Skyler said, nodding as she took a sip of the coffee.

Jessie watched the exchange, thinking that the two women seemed to have an easy relationship. She had no way of knowing how uneasy things had been at times, at that moment, however, they seemed to really connect.

Everyone sat for a while, chatting about this and that. Skyler stayed silent for the most part, only adding a comment here or there.

"We were talking about Benny's crush on you before you got up," Jams told Skyler.

"Really?" Skyler asked, raising an eyebrow at her partner.

Jams chuckled, nodding.

"We thought he was sweet on you from the way he talked about you," Jessie said.

Skyler smiled softly. "Yeah, that was a tough one," she said, then looking at Jessie she continued. "He brought me flowers one morning and that's when I knew for sure that he liked me in that way. I felt so bad that I had to sit him down and explain to him that I was gay. He took it like a trooper. And he told me that if I ever changed my mind, he wanted to be first in line."

That had everyone at the table laughing.

"That's my boy!" Bill Senior said, smiling proudly.

"He eventually told us that you were gay," Jessie said, "but he never stopped talking about what a great pilot you were, and how lucky he felt getting to be part of your crew."

Skyler nodded, looking affected by what Jessie was saying. "I loved that kid," she said simply. She looked at Benny's parents then, and knew she needed to tell them the story.

"We were on a mission…" she began, feeling Devin's hand on her leg squeeze gently, Skyler covered Devin's hand with hers, giving it a squeeze. "…that day, we thought it was going to be quick. We just needed to get some intel on an area they were looking at… we never even saw the group that shot us down," she said, haunted. "They took out our tail rotor, I tried to control the crash, and we almost had it, but we got hit again. That's when we went down, but we bounced. We bounced hard..." She was re-living it all over again.

She let out an audible breath, struggling to hold back the tears that wanted to come, but knowing she wouldn't get through this if she let herself cry. "Radar was killed on impact." She gritted her teeth to maintain her control. "Benny was hurt, bad, but he was alive."

"And you?" Jessie asked.

Skyler took a deep breath, blowing it out. "I broke a couple of ribs, punctured a lung," she said as if the injuries were minor. "Jams banged his head up pretty good."

Jessie nodded, having wanted to know that information. The Army hadn't told her about Skyler or Jams injuries, only that two members of the crew had been killed, including her son. She'd seen that Skyler and Jams had been wearing bandages and such at the funeral, but her focus had been on Billy.

"We hadn't made it out of the helicopter, we barely had a chance to figure out that Radar was gone, and Billy was hurt, when they got to us. They shot me, they shot Jams twice."

"They?" Bill Senior asked, his tone horrified, because he was pretty sure what she meant.

"Insurgents."

Bill Senior closed his eyes, taking that in, his son had been taken prisoner. Then he looked at Skyler, suddenly realizing what that probably had meant for a woman.

Skyler saw the look in Bill Senior's eyes and swallowed convulsively nodding to him.

"Oh God in Heaven…" Bill whispered.

Jessie looked over at her husband, not having grasped what her husband had.

"A woman in hostile custody," Bill said, taking his wife's hands in his, "isn't exactly treated gently."

Jessie's mouth dropped opened in horror, as she looked over at Skyler with eyes the size of saucers. "Oh my lord…"

Skyler drew in a breath, blowing it out as she stared down at the table. "They'd tied Jams up, because he was semi-conscious, but Benny was out, and I tried to stay quiet, not to scream. But then he woke up, and I tried to tell him to stand down," she said, her voice breaking on the last, her look was miserable as she lifted her eyes to them, tears sliding down her cheeks. "But he wouldn't listen…" She shook her head slowly. "They stabbed him… before I could do anything…"

"That's when she let them have it," Jams said, looking over at his partner, his lips twisted in anger. "She grabbed the knife that the guy had used, and she used it to stab him in the throat, then she took out the other two before they could blink." His tone of voice was proud, even as tears were in his eyes. "I didn't even have time to help her."

"You were barely conscious, and tied up," Skyler told him, her voice stronger in her need to support him.

Jams nodded, accepting her statement.

"I got over to Benny," Skyler said, "he was still alive at that point, but I could see he wasn't going to make it…" She shook her head sadly. "I held his hand, I told him that I loved him, and that he was going to be okay…" her voice trailed. In her mind she was watching the life leave Benny's eyes for the hundredth time.

"She's the one that got us all to the truck outside, and back to base," Jams said.

Jessie stared at Skyler through her tears, unable to believe what she'd heard. How did anyone handle so much?

"I'm sorry," Skyler whispered, "I'm sorry I couldn't save him."

Jessie got out of her chair and walked over to where Skyler sat, taking Skyler's head in her hands and looking her in the eye.

"You have nothing to be sorry for," she told Skyler. "Our son loved you, and nothing would have stopped him from trying to save you from that fate."

"If I hadn't been there…" Skyler said, "a damned woman in Iraq…"

"You can't do that to yourself," Bill Senior said, reaching over to clasp Skyler's shoulder. "You were there like everyone else, and you were serving your country, just like my boy was."

Skyler nodded, tears still falling silently. Jessie hugged Skyler to her, her tears flowing as well.

Devin watched the scene with tears streaming down her face, knowing what it was costing Skyler to relieve that time, but also knowing that it was what she needed to do. It made Devin sick to hear the details of what had happened, but she wouldn't have wanted Skyler to go through this without her.

It was a while before everyone was done crying. Even Sebastian had sat quietly, listening to his sister's story again, and feeling his insides tie into knots. At one point, Skyler reached over and took his hand, squeezing it. He grinned at his sister, nodding.

"I think we all need a good ride," Bill Senior said finally.

Everyone started to laugh.

In the end, that's what they did, took a good long ride around the ranch. That night they had dinner, and then Jessie and Bill walked them out to their car.

Jessie hugged, Skyler, thanking her again for everything.

Bill Senior gave Skyler a hug and then a hard look. "You have to let this go now. You have to let him go."

Skyler grimaced sadly, thinking about her dream, but nodded.

The sun was just setting in the sky, and the last ray of sunshine seemed to choose the perfect moment to shine down on them. Skyler smiled, thinking it was Benny telling her goodbye.

Hugging Devin to her side, she smiled, and whispered, "Bye Benny."

She knew that she would carry Benny in her heart forever, but it was time to let him go… blowing her breath out slowly… she let him go.

Epilogue

Devin woke Skyler up on Christmas Eve, Skyler's birthday.

"Always waking me up on my birthday," Skyler said, grinning as she rubbed her eyes and sat up.

"I've got a surprise for you."

"Another trip to Vegas?"

"Nope."

Walking over to the door, Devin opened it, and in bounded a black and white husky pup. The puppy jumped up onto the bed, and straight into Skyler's arms, licking her eagerly.

"Oh, my God…" Skyler said, half laughing as she tried to stave off the puppy's attention.

Devin watched, grinning. "Sandy said you might be able to train the puppy to help with the PTSD."

Skyler nodded, even as she smiled at the dog's antics. Reaching out she turned the tag around on the collar. It read, "Benny." Skyler chuckled, as she looked back at Devin.

"I thought 'cause of the blue eyes," Devin said.

"It's perfect, thank you," Skyler said, leaning in to kiss her softly on the lips.

The rest of the day was spent getting everything they needed to make Benny a permanent part of the family. Skyler had moved in with Devin two months earlier, and things had been going very smoothly. After the visit to Texas, Skyler had been more determined to get her life back on track. She had regular appointments with Sandy, and felt like she was making good progress, as did Sandy.

They were eating dinner later that evening, when Skyler got a text.

"Damn," Skyler said, looking at her phone.

"What?"

"Gotta go in."

"Okay."

Skyler left the house a little while later, kissing Devin, and giving Benny a good head rub.

Skyler didn't get home until two o'clock in the morning. She showered and crawled into bed beside Devin, having to maneuver around a firmly ensconced Benny, who wagged his tail at her and licked her hand. Leaning over, she kissed Benny on the head, then moved to kiss Devin on the cheek before she settled down to sleep.

The next morning, Christmas morning, Devin woke to find that Skyler had come in sometime during the night. She figured it had been late. Getting out of bed she went about her morning, letting Benny out to go potty and feeding him, as well as making some breakfast for her and Skyler.

It was noon before Skyler stirred, and even then, Devin found her lying in bed staring up at the ceiling.

"Good morning," Devin said from the doorway.

She grinned at Benny who'd found his way back into the bedroom and now lay protectively next to Skyler. Benny issued a sound that sounded like "aroo!" at Devin.

"And good morning again to you," Devin said, talking to the dog.

She moved to lie down next to Skyler, kissing her on the lips as she did.

"So, how'd it go last night?" Devin asked.

"Ugh," Skyler said, rolling her eyes, "I didn't get home till about two."

"And how did it go?" Devin asked again.

Skyler grinned at her. "Three people, mom and two kids, one was a baby."

"Wow! And they're all okay?"

"Yep, minor scratches and stuff, but good otherwise. Their car is totaled, but thank God for car seats and airbags, they did their jobs."

"And you did yours," Devin put in.

"Yes."

"How old was the baby?"

"The little one…" Skyler said, thinking, "I dunno, maybe a couple of months, it was tiny."

"They're like that when they're little."

"Do tell…" Skyler said, narrowing her eyes at Devin.

"So, what about that?"

"What about what?" Skyler asked, surprised by the change in direction.

"Babies," Devin said.

"What about babies?" Skyler asked, looking befuddled.

Devin dropped her eyes from Skyler's for a moment, picking at the sheet. "Did you ever want a baby?" she asked, her tone falsely light.

Skyler moved her head, to get under Devin's eyes. "A baby?"

"Yeah," Devin said, looking at her again, "I mean, did you ever think about having kids."

Skyler looked pensive for a long minute, then looked back at Devin. "How would that kind of thing go?"

It was Devin's turn to be taken aback, she'd expected a yes or no answer. She shrugged, going back to picking at the sheet and not looking at Skyler. "Well, using artificial insemination…"

"Babe, I know how lesbians have babies," Skyler said, her grin wry. "I meant in our case."

Devin pressed her lips together. Skyler could see that she was nervous about the topic.

"I was thinking that I'd be the one to get pregnant," Devin said. "You wouldn't have to, or anything… and I was thinking that maybe we could get Sebastian to donate sperm, so the baby would have your DNA too…" her voice trailed off as she realized she was getting ahead of herself. Skyler hadn't even said she'd ever wanted kids.

Looking at Skyler again, she could see the skeptical look on Skyler's face.

"I don't know babe…." Skyler said, sounding doubtful. "I mean… I'm kinda traditional when it comes to this kind of stuff."

"Traditional?" Devin repeated her look shocked.

"Yeah," Skyler said, her look apologetic.

"Like a mom and a dad, traditional?" Devin asked then, her voice reflecting her amazement over Skyler's response.

Skyler didn't answer, just shrugging in response.

There was a long moment of silence, where Devin searched desperately for something to say, even as she'd begun to wonder if she knew Skyler as well as she thought she did.

"Maybe," Skyler said then, as she stretched, sliding her hand under her pillow, "if you wore this..." She pulled her hand out of the pillow and holding up a ring between her thumb and forefinger. "I could get behind the idea."

Devin stared at the ring, her mouth open in shock, looking at Skyler she saw the grin and the sparkle in her light blue-green eyes. Then she narrowed her eyes at Skyler.

"Are you asking me something?"

Skyler started to chuckle at the look on Devin's face. "Yes," she said, smiling now. "Devin, will you marry me?"

Devin blew her breath out, giving Skyler a scathing look. "I should say no, just to get back at you."

Skyler started to put the ring away, but Devin grabbed it. "But I'm saying yes!" she said then, laughing as Skyler put it on her finger.

Devin looked at the ring for a long moment; it wasn't a traditional ring at all. It was a channel ring set with emerald baguettes with one large marquise cut emerald in the center.

"Not exactly a traditional ring," Devin commented.

"You're not really a traditional girl," Skyler countered.

"Were you planning on giving this to me all along?"

"Yeah."

"But you let me think that you thought I was crazy?"

"Hey, I didn't know we were going to be having a baby conversation this morning," Skyler said, holding up her hand defensively.

"True," Devin said, looking down at the ring, then looking at Skyler. "But do you want a baby?"

"With you?"

"Yeah."

"Abso-freakin-lutely!" Skyler replied, as she leaned in to kiss Devin deeply.

Benny added his two cents, by nuzzling between the two of them, and licking them both excitedly on the face.

The world was right again, and it was a wonderful day.

34017236R00148

Printed in Great Britain
by Amazon